DEAD MAN'S CHEST

Concept and Design: Lance Hawvermale

Writing Team: Lance Hawvermale, Rob Mason, Robert Hunter, Patrick Goulah, Greg Ragland, Matt McGee, Chris Bernhardt, Casey W. Christofferson, Chad Coulter, Skeeter Green, and Travis Hawvermale

Additional Contributers: Erica Balsley, Lindsey Barrentine, Jay Decker, Rachel Mason, and Nadine Oatmeyer

Swords & Wizardry Conversion: Jeff Harkness

Developers: Erical Balsley, Bill Webb, and Skeeter Green

Producer: Bill Webb

Editors: Jeff Harkness, Pat Lawinger, John, Ling, Edwin Nagy, and Karen McDonald

Art Direction: Casey Christofferson

Cover Art: Adrian Landeros

Interior Art: Julio De Cravahlo, Brian LeBlance, and Eric Lofgren

Layout and Graphic Design: Charles A. Wright

Fantasy Grounds Conversion: Michael W. Potter

©2019 Frog God Games. All rights reserved. Reproduction without the written permission of the publisher is expressly forbidden. Frog God Games and the Frog God Games logo is a trademark of Frog God Games. All characters, names, places, items, art and text herein are copyrighted by Frog God Games, Inc. The mention of or reference to any company or product in these pages is not a challenge to the trademark or copyright concerned.

Product Identity: The following items are hereby identified as Frog God Games LLC's Product Identity, as defined in the Open Game License version 1.0a, Section 1(e), and are not Open Game Content: product and product line names, logos and identifying marks including trade dress; artifacts; creatures; characters; stories, storylines, plots, thematic elements, dialogue, incidents, language, artwork, symbols, designs, depictions, likenesses, formats, poses, concepts, themes and graphic, photographic and other visual or audio representations; names and descriptions of characters, spells, enchantments, personalities, teams, personas, likenesses and sptecial abilities; places, locations, environments, creatures, equipment, magical or supernatural abilities or effects, logos, symbols, or graphic designs; and any other trademark or registered trademark clearly identified as Product Identity. Previously released Open Game Content is excluded from the above list.

ADVENTURES WORTH WINNING

FROG GOD GAMES IS:

Bill Webb, Matthew J. Finch, Zach Glazar, Charles A. Wright, Edwin Nagy, Mike Badalato

FROG GOD GAMES

ISBN: 978-1-62283-801-1

TABLE OF CONTENTS

DEAD MAN'S CHEST
INTRODUCTION

No place offers more adventure than the ocean. No dungeon is as deep, no jungle as full of exotic and dangerous life. Most folk spend their lives on dry ground, unaware that entire civilizations thrive beneath the waves, sometimes far more ancient and steeped in mystery than any of the world's surface. Though characters have long grown familiar with the air-breathing world above, seldom do they venture into the depths, and when they do, they discover wonders they never dreamed existed. The ocean environment is radically different from the surface world, in at least three very important ways: an insufficiency or complete absence of sunlight, the ever-increasing ambient pressure, and

the fact that water rather than air is the omnipresent medium for respiration, movement, and all other activities. Because of these and other factors, the ocean offers a venue for adventure that is at once alien and appealing. Strange things exist down there, as perilous as they are compelling.

But the water's surface is also a world unto itself. Great ships vie for control of the trading lanes. Dangerous reefs protect lost islands full of treasures yet unearthed. *Dead Man's Chest* lays bare the ocean. Within these pages you'll find rules variants to add to your game, many new spells, and wondrous items, but also information on the science of oceanography.

CHAPTER 1: AN OCEANOGRAPHY PRIMER

The ocean contains a variety of natural occurrences that can enliven any campaign. You shouldn't be dependent solely on monstrous encounters to make your character's life eventful on the high seas. This chapter reveals a short summary on many oceanic features, enabling you to present the characters with a more realistic description of the world that they will find themselves in.

Each entry also explains how best to use that particular feature in your own campaign.

MID-OCEAN RIDGE

The mid-ocean ridge is the region along the ocean floor where new seafloor is created. This typically takes place near the center of an ocean basin, though it exists in any location where two ocean plates spread apart from one another. Mid-ocean ridges are featured throughout the world, stretching over 40,000 miles in length. Their pattern winds across the globe in a fashion that is often likened to the seams of a baseball. They appear as mountainous formations or merely as mild swells upon the seafloor up to 2,400 miles wide. Their crest is marked with a V-shaped depression running throughout its range, up to a mile deep and 10 to 20 miles wide. This rift valley is actually a volcanic fissure from which the new seafloor extends from below gradually over time.

The origin of the seafloor naturally begins beneath the surface. Within the rift where the two tectonic plates diverge, the reduction of pressure affecting the mantle allows the rock of the asthenosphere (the upper layer of the mantle) to rise and melt. The upwelling leads to the formation of magma chambers just beneath the mid-ocean ridge, acting as focal reservoirs of the material needed to produce new ocean crust. Molten rock from the depths of the magma chamber gradually hardens, producing several miles of coarse rock. Vertical sheets of magma from within the chamber rise up through fissures in the overlying crust, creating dikes. Portions of this uprising magma will break through to the surface, oozing along the seafloor exterior. The outer layer of the surface lava solidifies immediately in the near-freezing seawater, forming a pillowed layer of volcanic basalt — the surface of the new seafloor.

The mid-ocean ridge axis is marked with deep, jagged indentations known as fracture zones. These appear in frequent intervals across the ridge, offsetting its crest up to hundreds of miles in either direction. The fracture zones appearing between two offset segments of the ridge are recognized as transform faults, and the fracture zones outside of these segments are simply remnants of the plate's movement over millions of years. The segmented ridge is generally widest and highest in the middle of the offset, and slimmest and shortest near the ends, and is believed to occur due to an interaction between fracturing of the seafloor and magma accumulation.

Another feature of interest to be found on the mid-ocean ridge is hot springs, or hydrothermal vents. Hydrothermal vent fields are areas of underwater geysers that form in places along the mid-ocean ridge axis. When seawater creeps into deep cracks and fissures found in the flanks of the ridge, it reacts with the hot volcanic rock, chemically altering and heating it up to temperatures reaching 700° Fahrenheit. This superheated fluid rises, dissolving metals found within the rocks on its way back up to the surface. Continuous streams of thick black or white immensely hot fluid projects straight up through vents in the surface, showering the surroundings with precipitated minerals.

The fluids in vents known as black smokers precipitate so quickly as they cool in the seawater that the metal sulfides form solid, smokestack structures, typically a couple of stories high (the largest ever discovered is 160 feet tall). In regions where the altered seawater is substantially cooled before reaching the surface, the ejected fluid is usually spread out among numerous vents in the area and takes on a diffused, clear glow. These diffuse vents are often found among larger more focused black smokers.

Life on the ocean floor is known for its scarcity, but hydrothermal vent fields are packed with an abundance and variety of life in one of the most volatile and unlikely of places. Organisms such as tubeworms, mussels, clams, and crustaceans gather or attach themselves near vents in incredibly dense clumps. However, it is the sulfur-eating bacteria found around and inside those creatures that grants them nourishment. The sulfide-oxidizing bacteria convert the vent chemicals into energy for the organisms through a process called chemosynthesis. This localized ecosystem is one of few known to exist independent of sunlight and photosynthesis.

USING MID-OCEAN RIDGES IN THE CAMPAIGN

In campaign worlds, mid-ocean ridges should be an important feature of the ocean. They mark the birthplace of the seafloor, directly influencing the geography of the planet, and provide an unlikely though successful site for life. The ridge shapes and sizes vary slightly from ocean to ocean, as does their productivity. In certain areas of the mid-ocean ridge, profuse magma accumulation beneath the ridge may produce large volcanic islands bisected by the active spreading ridge, such as Iceland in the North Atlantic.

Given the importance and regional nature of the mid-ocean ridge, implementing them into your game should prove simple and rewarding. Moderately intelligent ocean life dwelling on or near the ocean floor would certainly hold some opinion of it. Whether or not they fully understand its significance and true nature, some races may believe it to be sacred territory, or even a place where the deities exercise their direct will through volatile bursts of eruption. Denizens of the deep might even go to war over the rights to claim such land for spiritual and ancestral beliefs and practice. Races like sahuagin place great value on these areas. Furthermore, in specific places along the mid-ocean ridge, valuable minerals and metals could be discharged into the ocean in addition to seafloor, ripe for harvesting, and for conflict.

OCEAN FLOOR

From the time of its birth within the mid-ocean ridge, the young ocean floor is in constant motion. From the flanks of the ridge axis, gravity causes the new crust to fall away, accentuating the peaks of the ridge formation. Continuing, it becomes colder and contracts with time, growing denser and settling further. Sediment accumulation obscures its rock and hill-laden topography gradually, resulting in vast flatlands. Eventually, its existence will conclude in the inevitable return to the planet's mantle in deep trenches, some thousand miles away and millions of years later.

The ocean floor is a place of mystery. By its very nature it is not prone to exploration. At the average depth of the ocean floor at 13,000 feet, near-freezing seafloor water, crushing water pressure, and complete lack of sunlight make for a very uninviting environment. For these reasons, ocean floor exploration has been a slow and educating process. The topography of the ocean floor is every bit as varied as the land we're more familiar with. Stretching flatlands, peaking mountains, rolling hills, and plummeting canyons are all common ocean floor features. But as is often the case, the features that characterize the ocean have the tendency to be larger in scale, more severe, and more frequent than on land. In addition to the mid-ocean ridge and ocean trenches (both explained in detail elsewhere within the chapter), the following ocean floor features are of special significance:

Abyssal Hills. The abyssal hills emerge in the wake of seafloor spreading at the mid-ocean ridge. They are composed most generally in linear rows stretching parallel to the spreading ridge axis, appearing as fractured, elongated peaks up to over 3,000 feet high and about six to 12 miles across. These hills are the most prominent geologic feature of the planet's surface. It is generally agreed that they are caused by an interaction of the faulting and eruptions taking place within the mid-ocean ridge axis. However, little of their formation and development is well understood.

Abyssal Plains. The abyssal plains are the flat regions of the ocean floor, constituting roughly half of the planet's topography. In fact, there is no flatter location on the plant, with a gradient no greater than 0.05 degrees. They are produced when the rocky terrain of the abyssal hills is obscured by sediment accumulation over the course of millions of years. The most significant contributor to the abyssal plains' flatness is the submarine flow of density-heavy currents called turbidity currents. These currents are basically underwater sediment avalanches, generated by earthquakes or simply acting as continuations of enduring river outlets. They transport mostly terrigenous (land originating) sediment from its settled location along the continental shelf to the continental slope and into the deep sea.

Sediment composition is varied throughout the ocean, based largely on a particular basin's history and location. The most abundant sediment composition is comprised of assorted clays, silts, and sands originating from land, metal-rich sediments, pebbles, and stone from the spreading ridges, and oozes consisting of calcareous and siliceous skeletal remains. On average, the thickness of sediment cover on the ocean floor is over half a mile. Typically, it is thickest near continental masses and thinnest near the center of an ocean basin, but other circumstances impact its accumulation. For instance, the Pacific Ocean's immense size places the inner regions of its basin out of reach from turbidity currents and most wind-carried sediments. In addition, its basin is nearly surrounded by hundreds of deep ocean trenches that funnel and trap a great deal of the sediments within their depths. As such, the abyssal hills comprise approximately three-quarters of the Pacific. The floor of the Atlantic Ocean, much smaller and with few trenches of significant size for sediments to escape, is nearly half-featured with abyssal hills.

Seamounts. Punctuating the ocean floor are seamounts, isolated seafloor volcanoes of heights greater than 600 miles (dwarfing Mount Everest's almost six-mile height). They are most often conical, and have a recessed caldera within their summit. Seamounts that have flattened tops due to excessive erosion caused by water currents are called guyots. Thousands of seamounts are on the ocean floor, and many serve as great habitats of life. Creatures classified as suspension feeders adorn the steep slopes of seamounts near the top to intercept organic matter passing by in the water currents. Various coral polyps, sponges, and xenophyophores (single celled creatures similar to fungi that can grow up to eight inches across) cling to seamounts to feed in this manner. Their presence also attracts other ocean wildlife. Seamounts are also larvae catchers; the very currents that provide food for seamount communities also provide for its continued population.

A small percentage of seamounts appear to have been created at the mid-ocean ridge. However, most are formed above regions known as hot spots, exceedingly hot locations within the mantle where plumes of magma have risen and melted through the oceanic lithosphere. The majority of these seamounts are no longer volcanically active, having been carried away from the magma source by the movement of the ocean plate. The seamounts created by exceptionally prolific hotspots break the surface of the ocean, often producing a chain of volcanic islands. As the oceanic crust glides over the excessive hot spot, one by one and oldest to youngest, an arcing trail of volcanic islands forms. A notable real-life example of this is the Hawaiian Islands. Chains of these seamount islands can extend many thousands of miles.

Life on the ocean floor — its presence, diversity, and development — is constantly being redefined. As we further explore the great depths of the ocean, the perceptions of a stale and stagnant seafloor largely devoid of life are being shattered. Despite the relative scarcity of life to be found there, it is startlingly diverse. The possible number of species is projected to soar well beyond one million, and possibly possessing

more biodiversity than the rain forest. Among the countless species of life inhabiting the deep seas are grenadier fish, slime-secreting eel-like hagfish, echinoderms such as sea cucumbers and brittle stars, and various species of crustaceans and invertebrates.

The primary source of food for many of these bottom-dwellers is organic debris that falls from the surface waters. This organic detritus, or marine snow, consists of microscopic, one-celled plant (phytoplankton) and animal (zooplankton) remains, along with various dissolved particulates that have clumped together into tiny flakes. Throughout the oceans, marine snow falls, raining down in sporadic pulses. In the summer, the spring-born plankton die in great numbers and immerse the ocean in a blizzard of organic matter, blanketing some spots on the ocean floor in a thick green blanket of dead matter. This, in addition to the rare arrival of whole animal carcasses, is what feeds the majority of the ocean floor life.

USING THE OCEAN FLOOR IN THE GAME

Adventure in the deep ocean should be highlighted with a constant hint of danger and suspense to keep the characters on edge. Those brave enough to defy the pulverizing pressure, near-freezing water, and utter blackness of the sea at those depths should be rewarded with an eventful experience. Whether it's subterranean monsters burrowing within the mud-packed sediment floor of the abyssal plains; ancient civilizations living in the abyssal hills, forced to migrate towards the mid-ocean ridge as their habitat is slowly consumed with sediments; or perhaps even elemental-driven turbidity currents sweeping throughout the sea like colossal sand storms, the ocean floor should provide plenty of excitement, and endless possibilities in your campaign.

REEFS

An important part of oceanic life, reefs are defined as elevated ridges along shallow places on the seafloor. Reefs are formed from creatures known as coral polyps, hence the popular name coral reef. Upon death, these tiny coral polyps leave behind hardened exoskeletons made of a calcareous (calcium-containing), stony material. These small bits of limestone, when combined with similar deposits from countless polyps, form the beautiful and labyrinthine structures that are coral reefs.

Depending on the number of polyps that die in the area, coral reefs grow at rates between one to 40 inches each year. Coral reefs are found exclusively in tropical regions of the ocean, never beyond 30 degrees north or south of the planet's equator and never in waters cooler than 61° Fahrenheit. Two primary types of coral exist — hard and soft. Categories of hard coral include brain coral and elkhorn coral, both of which have hard limestone frames. Soft corals such as sea fingers and sea whips do not form reefs.

Most campaign worlds boast at least three different kinds of coral reefs, though there is no limit on the variety of reef that can appear in a fantasy setting. One such example is listed below, along with the three typical types of reefs.

Barrier Reefs. These reefs always run parallel to the shoreline, but several yards out and separated by a lagoon. Because these reefs form a kind of protective palisade around the beach, they are known as barrier reefs.

Coral Atolls. These are rings of coral atop old, sunken volcanoes. Coral atolls begin as fringe reefs surrounding volcanic islands, but when the island sinks, the reef keeps growing and is classified as a coral atoll. Horseshoe-shaped collections of coral, atolls form rings around small lagoons that fill the caldera of inactive volcanoes.

Fringing Reefs. Running directly along the coastline, the fringing reefs are found built close to the continental shelf in the shallow waters near shore.

Spherical Reef. One example of the kind of reef found in a fantasy world is the spherical reef. Also known as reef globes, these huge structures of coral are formed into great spheres by some unknown natural process. The walls of the reef globe are hard enough that the spheres can act as a temporary shelter for marine travelers.

Regardless of the exact nature of the reef, all such coral mazes are robust ecosystems supporting a variety of marine life. The reef's far layer consists of the living polyps, while below them are the calcareous reef framework, containing filamentous green algae. These algae provide nourishment for many of the animals that make their home in or near the reef. Fish and other creatures abound. A brief list of a reef's inhabitants includes the following: sponges, nudibranchs, reef sharks, groupers, clown fish, eels, snappers, jellyfish, anemones, sea stars, crabs, shrimps, lobsters, sea snakes, snails, octopi, nautilus, and clams.

USING REEFS IN THE GAME

Coral reefs make excellent sites for exotic adventure. Imagine a villain's underwater lair constructed from confusing coral passages. Spherical reefs can serve as hideouts for all manners of creatures, or hauled onto shore to use as part of an NPC's elaborate home. The stereotypical dungeon maze can take on a new form when made of coral; the winding coral corridors can present characters with a challenging labyrinth to solve. Reefs are notorious haunts for many dangerous beasts, such as eels, sharks, and octopi. Societies of sea elves can use coral to make armor, weapons, and other trade goods. Reefs are also known to conceal sunken ships beneath their protective arms of coral.

TECTONIC PLATES

The surface of the planet is essentially a rigid shell, a layer of thick rock comprised of continental or oceanic crust along with the uppermost portion of the mantle. This layer of the planet is known as the lithosphere. The oceanic lithosphere is on average six miles thick, while the continental lithosphere can be up to 60 miles thick. It is broken up into a dozen or more slabs or plates, known commonly as tectonic plates, which move and interact in relation to one another as they glide upon the asthenosphere, the partially molten rock region of the planet's mantle. The size and position of these tectonic plates are constantly changing, though only at rates of inches per year.

Tectonic plates interact with one another in several different ways, and the results of these interactions have a severe impact upon the topography and geology of the planet. In divergent boundaries, plates pull away from each other, creating new crust in the process. Since the size of the planet does not change, older crust must be destroyed simultaneously as new crust is formed. This occurs in the areas known as convergent boundaries, where two tectonic plates commit a slow collision. Transform boundaries, or transform-fault boundaries, are where two lithospheric plates simply glide or shift past the other.

Tectonic activity is never more evident, nor more crucial, than in the ocean. Geology occurs foremost at plate boundaries, and the plate boundaries of the ocean floor are of particular consequence to the rest of the planet as seismic and volcanic events occurring anywhere on the globe can be traced to activity at an ocean plate boundary. Furthermore, the phenomenon of seafloor spreading in divergent boundaries and the imminent result of ocean floor subduction in convergent boundaries points directly toward the composition and layout of the rest of the planet's surface.

USING TECTONIC ACTIVITY IN THE GAME

Tectonic plates are the origin of many large-scale events on any planet. Continental shelves are constantly moving — and sometimes this movement results in the release of a monster that had been contained for millennia deep in the crust of the earth. An NPC magic-user who wants to wreak havoc on the world above could cause a great explosion at the juncture of two lithospheric plates, resulting in massive land shifts. The movement of the plates can result in tidal waves and earthquakes. Seeing this, it's no surprise that powerful NPCs might contrive to take control of certain points on the ocean floor, places where they can use their magic to command tectonic activity.

TIDES AND WAVES

So much depends upon the tides. As one of the most fundamental aspects of oceanography, the importance of tides and tidal activity cannot be overstated. Without the constant movement of the tides, life below the surface would be greatly different, as would the lives of those dependent upon the incoming and outgoing waters along the coast. Any capable sailor is well-versed in tidal lore. The study of the nature of tides involves unraveling some of the core tenets of the universe, namely mass and gravity. Quite simply, tides are the occasional rise and fall of a planet's waters, including oceans, seas, and bays. This constant up-and-down motion is due directly to the gravitational forces exerted upon the planet by the sun and moon.

Lunar pull accounts for most of the tidal activity on the planet. In a game world that has no moon, or on a planet with multiple moons, the tides will behave differently depending on the amount of gravitational pull being exerted at any one time. On an earth-like planet, two "high water" and two "low water" periods occur every lunar day. This rising and falling of water results in lateral water movements called tidal currents (not to be confused with ocean currents). Tidal currents flow in a shoreward or upstream direction during high water then reverses flow during low water.

Waves are the result of the wind. Generally speaking, the greater the wind speed, the higher the waves. Note that waves do not move horizontally, but only up and down. Another type of wave, the tsunami, can cause vast and terrible damage to structures when it crashes upon the shore. Tsunamis are not caused by tides, but rather by tectonic activity such as earthquakes and undersea volcanoes.

WAVE HEIGHT TABLE (DAY)

| 1d00 | Height in feet | | | |
	Summer	Winter	Autumn	Spring
01–10	5	15	20	15
11–20	25	18	20	15
21–30	42	20	15	35
31–40	20	35	15	25
41–50	18	10	5	22
51–60	35	18	20	15
61–70	15	30	10	22
71–80	17	25	20	10
81–90	45	20	30	15
91–00	10	10	25	20

	Height in feet			
1d100	Summer	Winter	Autumn	Spring
01–10	25	18	25	15
11–20	42	20	20	35
21–30	20	35	15	25
31–40	18	10	5	22
41–50	35	18	20	15
51–60	15	30	10	22
61–70	17	25	20	10
71–80	45	20	30	15
81–90	10	10	25	20
91–00	5	15	20	15

USING TIDES AND WAVES IN THE GAME

Tides can be used to reveal or conceal sunken ships, the entrances to hidden lairs, or other things. Waves can make life miserable for anyone trying to travel across the open sea. Refer to the Wave Height table for a quick way to determine wave height. Roll 1d00 and consult either the day or night portion of the chart.

Big waves can cause trouble for those aboard ships. The Wave Effects table shows what happens when waves of a certain size wash over the sides, or gunwales, of ships.

The following are guidelines for using the table.

Wave Size. Compare the wave height from the Wave Height table to the height of the ship's gunwale to determine "wave size." This is the amount by which the wave is taller than the ship's side.

Saving Throw Modifier. Anyone forced to make a saving throw for any reason does so at a penalty when large waves wash over the ship.

Wave Effects. Any of these effects can be resisted with a Strength saving throw, the DC is indicated in the final column.

Knocked Prone. Creatures who fail their save are knocked prone by the force of the wave and swept in a random direction 1d6 feet.

Checked. Creatures who fail their save are unable to move against the force of the wave, and can take no action that round but that of stabilizing themselves.

Swept Overboard. Creatures who fail their save are knocked prone and carried 1d4 x 10 feet, taking 1d4 points damage per 10 feet traveled. If the distance traveled extends beyond the sides of the deck, the creature is tossed overboard.

TRENCHES

Ocean trenches are deep and narrow subterranean depressions within the ocean floor. They mark the deepest areas on the planet. It is in these trenches that the seafloor, now denser and well over 200 million years older, returns to the mantle where it is effectively recycled. Most often appearing adjacent to continental masses, their length can stretch up to thousands of miles. The depth of these trenches varies anywhere from the 20,000 feet necessary to generally be considered a trench, to over 35,000 feet.

Trenches form in the convergent plate boundaries known as subduction zones. General theory suggests that in these zones, an oceanic plate meets either another oceanic plate or continental plate and slides beneath it. The denser lithospheric ocean plate commits a slow plummet towards the mantle below, dragging the edge of the non-subducting plate down with it, producing the linear V-shaped trench. The dense lithosphere of older, thicker oceanic plates subducts quickly and steeply into the mantle, whereas the buoyant young lithosphere that is thinner and warmer bends slowly, creating a gentle trench slope.

The process of subduction has many consequences that impact the surrounding area, most notably the sweeping arcs of volcanoes. Over millions of years the convergence of the two plates leads to volcanic arc formations appearing on the overriding plate parallel to the subduction zone. As the descending oceanic plate lunges deeper towards the mantle below, it is subjected to greater pressure and rising temperatures. Eventually the surface water of the crust and hydrated minerals from within the basaltic portions of the subducting plate are discharged into the mantle portion of the overlying lithospheric plate. As the water interacts with the mantle, it decreases the mantle's melting temperature, allowing it to melt. A supply of the magma created rises through the crust of the overriding plate and forms the volcanic arc. When subduction zones involve two oceanic plates, the chains of volcanoes that break the ocean surface are called volcanic island arcs.

Other side effects characterize subduction zones. Interactions between the two converging plates generate some of the most seismically powerful earthquakes in the world. The plot of the subducting plate's ascension can be outlined by the seismic activity occurring deeper within the planet's mantle, several hundred thousand kilometers beneath the surface. The earthquakes focused along subduction zones tend to be cyclic and reactionary. Subduction zone earthquakes can also wreak havoc upon the coastal areas by causing the incredibly destructive waves called tsunamis. Tsunamis caused by the subduction zone earthquakes or earthquake-triggered submarine landslides can be catastrophic events, wiping out miles of coastlands.

Despite frequent sediment-dense avalanches along the slopes, ocean trenches provide fairly hospitable homes for creatures that are capable of withstanding the crushing water pressure. The water temperature and seawater salinity found in trenches is identical to the other areas of the deep sea, and sources of food tend to be slightly less scarce.

WAVE EFFECTS TABLE

Wave Force	Wave Size	Saving Throw Modifier	Wave Effect on Creatures
Light	0–2 feet	—	No effect
Moderate	3–5 feet	—	No effect
Strong	6–10 feet	−1	Knocked prone
Severe	11–30 feet	−2	Save or 50% chance of being swept overboard or knocked prone
Windstorm	31–50 feet	−4	Save or swept overboard (75%) or checked (25%)
Hurricane	51–100 feet	−6	Save or swept overboard (80%) or knocked prone (15%) or checked (5%)
Tornado	101+ feet	−8	Save or swept overboard

The trench profile traps generous amounts of organic matter within, distributing it down to even the deepest dwellers. Their proximity to the coasts also grants access to especially plankton-rich surface waters raining in nourishment from above. Additionally, cold methane seeps exist along the slopes of some trenches, packed with methane-eating bacteria that nourish the creatures nearby through chemosynthesis. Anemones, crustaceans, bristle worms, and most prominently, holothurians (sea cucumbers), make homes in ocean trenches.

USING TRENCHES IN THE GAME

In campaign worlds, trenches serve as perhaps the most remote locations of the planet — much like in reality. Very few would likely know of their existence, and fewer still would be willing to explore them. However, those that take the proper precautions and brave the seemingly bottomless depths of these trenches should have plenty of sights to see. Long-abandoned ruins of ancient civilizations found along the trench walls or partially submerged treasures of immeasurable worth within the sediment-filled valley are but a couple enticements. A strong downward suction could exist within the trench formation, or the subduction zone might cease and become dormant. This is to say nothing of the possibilities as to what terrors might exist within these fearsome depths.

Chapter 2: Underwater Adventuring

The oceans hide a world that most adventures and adventurers never explore. It is a world fraught with danger and discovery, mystery and the unknown.

Variants

Many factors come into play when the characters venture beneath the water's surface. The following are all self-contained variant rules that can be added to your campaign to add a sense of verisimilitude. This is not to say that it will add realism, but in a seafaring campaign, these rules attempt to address issue that might draw your players out of the story you are attempting to tell.

Feel free to modify them as you feel is appropriate for your campaign.

Swimming

A creature with a swimming speed does not need to worry overmuch about rough surf or strong currents, save for supernatural ones. A creature that lacks a swimming speed is at a distinct disadvantage while in water. The easiest way for a creature to gain a swimming speed is to use *polymorph self* but other magical items might grant the same ability. A creature without a swim speed can swim at half their normal walking speed in normal surf. They may need to make a saving throw to move forward in especially rough water.

Vision

Seeing underwater is a difficult question to address, and will need to be taken in two steps: available light and turbidity, or clarity of the water.

Sunlight

For the purposes of sunlight into the open ocean, the depths of the ocean are divided into three separate sections: the sunlight, twilight, and midnight zones. In the absence of sunlight — such as on a moonlit night — the ocean is complete darkness beneath 15 feet of water, and dim light to the surface.

The Sunlight (Euphotic) Zone. The sunlight zone occupies a depth down to 650 feet. Within this zone, sunlight allows vision to work normally absent any other conditions.

The Twilight (Dysphotic) Zone. The twilight zone occupies the deep from 650 feet down to 3,000 feet. In this zone, sunlight rapidly decreases and it is considered dim light absent any other conditions.

The Midnight (Aphotic) Zone. The midnight zone begins at 3,000 feet and continues to the bottom. In this zone, it is complete darkness.

Visibility

Water's visibility is based on its turbidity, or the measure of the relative clarity of the liquid medium. Unlike the diffusion of sunlight by the passage of water, this is when material affects how clear a body of water is by turning the water cloudy or opaque. A body of water's turbidity is always a function of external circumstance, such as the body of water's location or excessive churning of the water from storms.

An area of water's turbidity breaks down into four categories: low, medium, high, and occluded.

Low Turbidity

Areas of low turbidity have a visibility distance of 180 (4d8 x 10) feet. Creatures or objects beyond this distance are heavily obscured, and creatures beyond half that distance are lightly obscured. Areas of low turbidity are most commonly found in deep water and occasionally in tropical coastal areas.

Medium Turbidity

Areas of medium turbidity include sounds, bays, and coastal waters, caused by their relatively shallow depth and the sea currents which flow through them. An area of medium turbidity has a visibility distance of 90 (2d8 x 10) feet, beyond which creatures and objects are heavily obscured. Creature and objects are lightly obscured beyond half that distance.

High Turbidity

Rivers and harbors always have high turbidity. The areas have sediment and silt from river mouths, which cause creatures to be heavily obscured beyond 30 (1d6 x 10) feet, and lightly obscured beyond half that distance.

Occluded

Reserved for the most turbulent waters, occluded waters have a visibility distance of 10 (1d4 x 5) feet, beyond which creatures are heavily obscured. Creatures and objects are lightly obscured within half that distance. Areas of occluded visibility occur in the strongest currents, such as those churned by storms or underwater events like eruptions and earthquakes, like the turbidity currents that cross the abyssal plains.

Breathing

The most obvious way to handle breathing underwater is the *water breathing* spell. Its utility and breadth makes it a necessity in seafaring adventures. However, if a creature does not possess it or another feature that allows them to breathe underwater, you can utilize the following rules.

A creature can hold its breath for a number of minutes equal to one-quarter of its constitution score (rounded down, minimum of one minute) if a creature does nothing but swim in normal surf.

A creature that is holding its breath when it takes damage from any source must make a saving throw. On a failure, they exhale and run out of breath.

Pressure

Pressure is a function of a creature's depth, caused by the weight of the water above them. For creatures of the land, this is an unknown and dangerous world. A creature that strays too deep risks having their blood pushed from their veins and into their lungs, where they drown on it.

Depth Rating. A depth rating is a number of increments of 30 feet, and it is these ratings that determine how deep a creature can go before suffering from the effects of pressure. A creature's maximum depth rating is equal to their constitution score x 30. For example, a creature with a constitution of 10 can survive the pressure up to 300 feet without ill effects — assuming they have a source of magic or another feature that allows them to avoid drowning.

Once a creature reaches this depth, the effects of pressure become noticeable.

Water Breathing. A creature that can breathe water, either through magical or natural means, doubles their maximum depth rating.

Creatures. A creature that is native to aquatic environments, such as one that has a swim speed like the killer whale, also doubles their maximum depth rating. This is cumulative with the ability to breathe water natively.

Damage. A creature takes a cumulative 1d6 points of damage at the end of each of their turns for every 30 feet past their maximum depth rating. This has an effect on a creature's ability to hold their breath, as detailed above.

Pressure Summary

Creature Type	Depth Rating
Non-aquatic creature that can't breathe water	Constitution score x 30 ft.
Can breathe water *or* aquatic creature	Constitution score x 60 ft.
Can breathe water *and* aquatic creature	Constitution score x 120 ft.

Underwater Combat

The rules for underwater combat are fairly straightforward, but the following can add a bit of fun during combat.

Melee Weapon Attacks. While underwater, a creature that doesn't have a swimming speed (either naturally or granted by spells like *polymorph self*) suffers a –1 to-hit penalty unless the weapon is a dagger, javelin, short sword, spear, or trident.

Ranged Weapon Attacks. A creature takes a –4 to-hit penalty with a crossbow, net, or a weapon that is thrown like a javelin (including a spear, trident, or dart).

From Land to Sea. Creatures floating on the surface of the water can be targeted by attacks from creature above the surface normally. However, if a creature is fully submerged but still within sight, they gain a +1 armor class bonus to account for water's bending of light which obscures their vision. Any creature deeper than 10 feet gains a +2 armor class bonus.

Eric Lofgren

CHAPTER 3: WEATHER

The bulk of this chapter contains daily weather entries, small capsules that describe the weather for a particular day, including high and low temperatures, windspeed, and other events. Preceding this information, however, is a look at certain weather-related factors that impact the data in the daily weather entries.

TEMPERATURE

Temperature in the daily weather entries is listed in Fahrenheit and Celsius, with both highs and lows. For example, you might find this entry: Temp H 92/34 L 71/22. This means that the high temperature for that day will be 92° F or 34° C, with lows of 71° and 22°.

HUMIDITY AND WIND CHILL

Two factors that combine with temperature to cause misery to travelers are humidity and wind chill. Though it might actually be 85° F, a high humidity can make it feel like an unbearable 105° F, while a strong wind can drop that and make it feel like a comfortable 72° F. High humidity prohibits the body from being able to cool itself properly. Thus, the body perceives the temperature as being higher than it actually is. This perceived temperature is called the heat index. The daily weather entries show you the base high and low temperatures, but you may optionally alter these temperatures by adding the effects of humidity and wind chill. On warm days, roll on the Random Humidity Table to find the percentage of humidity. When humidity is 50% or higher, refer to the daily weather entry to find the day's high temperature, then use the Heat Index Table to see how hot a character feels in such conditions. On days where the cold can be a problem, read the windspeed in the daily weather entry, then refer to the Wind Chill Table on page 12.

TEMPERATURE EFFECTS

Extremely high and low temperatures have serious effects on characters who are unprotected from the elements. Some of these effects are detailed in the daily weather entries. Other effects include the following:

Temperature Below 40° F. An unprotected character must succeed on a saving throw each hour or take 1d6 points of cold damage. For each failed saving throw, subsequent saves are made with a cumulative –1 penalty. Characters wearing winter clothing need not make these checks.

Temperature Below 0° F. In conditions of severe cold or exposure, an unprotected character must make a saving throw once every 10 minutes or take 1d6 points of cold damage. For each failed saving throw, subsequent saves are made with a cumulative –1 penalty. Characters wearing winter clothing only need to make this check once per hour.

Temperature Below –20° F. Extreme cold forces unprotected characters to succeed on a saving throw every minute or take 1d6 points of cold damage. For each failed saving throw, subsequent saves are made with a cumulative –1 penalty. Characters wearing winter clothing only need to make this check every 30 minutes. Those failing their saving throw and wearing metal armor take an additional 1d6 points of cold damage and suffer a –1 penalty on attacks and saves until they doff the armor.

Temperature Above 90° F. A character in very hot conditions must succeed on a saving throw every hour or take 1d4 points of damage. For each failed saving throw, subsequent saves are made with a cumulative –1 penalty. Characters wearing heavy clothing or any sort of armor also take an additional –1 penalty on these checks.

Temperature Above 110° F. In severe heat, a character must succeed on a saving throw once every 10 minutes or take 1d4 points of damage. For each failed saving throw, subsequent saves are made with a cumulative –1 penalty. Characters wearing heavy clothing or any sort of armor also take an additional –1 penalty on these checks.

Temperature Above 140° F. Exposure to these temperatures requires that characters succeed on a saving throw every minute or take 1d6 points of damage. For each failed saving throw, subsequent saves are made with a cumulative –1 penalty. Characters wearing heavy clothing or any sort of armor also take an additional –1 penalty on these checks

RANDOM HUMIDITY

1d20	Arctic	Tropical	Temperate	Equatorial
1–2	10%	50%	10%	60%
3–6	10%	60%	20%	70%
7–10	20%	70%	30%	80%
11–14	30%	80%	40%	80%
15–18	40%	80%	50%	90%
19	50%	90%	60%	90%
20	50%	90%	70%	90%

HEAT INDEX TABLE

Temp.	50%	60%	70%	80%	90%
80	80	81	82	84	85
85	86	90	92	96	101
90	94	99	105	113	121
100	118	129	142	161	178

WIND

A typical entry for wind might look like this: Wind — 10–15 mph. This means that the wind is moving between 10 and 15 miles per hour. Note that this is the base windspeed. You may, at your discretion, roll 4d6 and add the result to the base windspeed.

Wind Direction. To determine the direction of the wind, consult the Wind Direction table.

RANDOM WIND DIRECTION

Roll 1d4, then 1d8

	1–2		3–4	
1d8	Wind Direction	1d8	Wind Direction
1	NNE	1	SSW
2	NE	2	SW
3	ENE	3	WSW
4	E	4	W
5	ESE	5	WNW
6	SE	6	NW
7	SSE	7	NNW
8	S	8	N

Temp. (F)	Wind Speed (mph)											
	5	10	15	20	25	30	35	40	45	50	55	60
40	36	34	32	30	29	28	28	27	26	26	25	25
35	31	27	25	24	23	22	21	20	19	19	18	17
30	25	21	19	17	16	15	14	13	12	12	11	10
25	19	15	13	11	9	8	7	6	5	4	4	3
20	13	9	6	4	3	1	0	−1	−2	−3	−3	−4
15	7	3	0	−2	−4	−5	−7	−8	−9	−10	−11	−11
10	1	−4	−7	−9	−11	−12	−14	−15	−16	−17	−18	−19
5	−5	−10	−13	−15	−17	−19	−21	−22	−23	−24	−25	−26
0	−11	−16	−19	−22	−24	−26	−27	−29	−30	−31	−32	−33
−5	−16	−22	−26	−29	−31	−33	−34	−36	−37	−38	−39	−40
−10	−22	−28	−32	−35	−37	−39	−41	−43	−44	−45	−46	−48
−15	−28	−35	−39	−42	−44	−46	−48	−50	−51	−52	−54	−55
−20	−34	−41	−45	−48	−51	−53	−55	−57	−58	−60	−61	−62
−25	−40	−47	−51	−55	−58	−60	−62	−64	−65	−67	−68	−69
−30	−46	−53	−58	−61	−64	−67	−69	−71	−72	−74	−75	−76
−35	−52	−59	−61	−68	−71	−73	−76	−78	−79	−81	−82	−84
−40	−57	−66	−71	−74	−78	−80	−82	−84	−86	−88	−89	−91
−45	−63	−72	−77	−81	−84	−87	−89	−91	−93	−95	−97	−98

DAILY WEATHER

The remainder of this chapter comprises daily weather entries. The information is broken into several parts. To determine daily weather, first find the current season (Spring, Summer, Autumn, Winter). Then find the appropriate terrain type (Tropical, Equatorial, Temperate, or Arctic). At this point, you can select from one of the following options: Rain/Day, Rain/Night, Dry/Day, or Dry/Night. It's up to you to decide whether it's day or night, but for purposes of rain, roll 1d20 and use the Precipitation at Sea table. Note that this table in no way represents realistic precipitation chances, but simply provides a ready means to determine random weather. Finally, roll 1d100 to find the exact weather entry for that day.

PRECIPITATION AT SEA

	Dry	Rain/Snow
Arctic Sea	1–6	7–20
Desert Coast	1–18	19–20
Jungle Coast	1–4	5–20
Swamp Coast	1–9	10–20
Temperate Sea	1–12	13–20
Tropical Sea	1–7	8–20

SUMMER

TROPICAL

Heatstroke is a risk for any who travel the warm regions of the world. Those exerting themselves must succeed on a saving throw for each hour of strenuous work or become exhausted (–1 to hit, damage and saves). For each cumulative hour of strenuous work, the save is made with a cumulative –1 penalty. Resting in shaded areas for 10 minutes per hour negates the –1 penalty for that hour. Spell components run a 10% chance of spoiling in humidity, if you determine they are subject to such damage.

RAIN/DAY

01–20	A gentle breeze blows, adding a pleasant cooling to the warm rain falling. Large drops patter along the deck, and occasional sunshine warms the deck, quickly evaporating the rain and adding to the humidity. A sticky aspect of the air grows throughout the day as the humidity rises. Sunlight glints off the water like numerous smaller suns, blinding those not ready for the effect. Waves are large in width but not in height and rock the ship with their passage. (Temp H 92/34 L 71/22, Wind — 10–15 mph.)
21–40	Steady rain pummels the ship and those on board, quickly soaking all equipment and people. The waves are sedated, rarely topping five feet, seemingly held down with the rain. The sun tries to pierce the cloud cover with its intense glare, only succeeding in raising the temperature. Wind is nonexistent, hammered to submission by the heavy rain (Temp H 91/33 L 80/27, Wind — 0–5 mph.)
41–60	Seemingly in rhythm with the lapping waves, periodic rain drops in vast amounts, quickly soaking all surfaces and washing away loose items. Between rainfalls, the sun attempts to burn away the moisture with blistering heat. Waves roll languidly, topping six feet in height but not steep enough to make more than an exaggerated rocking motion. The wind blows merrily, billowing out the sails of the ship and propelling the vessel over the large waves. (Temp H 89/32 L 71/22, Wind – 10–15 mph. Characters moving on deck during a deluge must succeed on a saving throw or be knocked prone and pushed 10 feet in a random direction.)
61–80	A drizzle of rain, sometimes hard and sometimes light, falls continuously throughout the day. All surfaces are thoroughly soaked and heavy with water. The warmth of the occasional sun is diminished slightly by the cool rain, keeping it tolerable for all involved. Waves are present but pose no real threat to the direction of the ship or her course. The wind blows constantly, keeping the sails full but not pushing the limit of its capabilities. (Temp H 87/31 L 78/26, Wind — 15–20 mph.)
81–00	Heavy rain from unseen clouds pummels the ship and those on deck. Waves like great gray-green boulders smashing against the ship every minute. The overhead clouds descend to a point where it seems the ship is in a large chamber. Wind hurtles against the vessel and its sail, trying to rip it from the mast and rigging. All loose items on deck vie for attention from the crashing waves or the blustery wind. (Temp H 91/33 L 80/27, Wind — 50–55 mph. Characters moving on deck must succeed on a saving throw each round or be knocked prone and pushed 10 feet in a random direction. All exposed areas of the ship are lightly obscured.)

RAIN/NIGHT

01–20	The cool of the night is accompanied by the patter of rain upon the deck. The humidity keeps the coolness of the night from being comfortable. The moon makes itself known through the clouds, illuminating a portion of the night sky to milky white. The waves crash against the hull as if trying to keep the ship from reaching its goal. The bounce of the ship as it passes over the waves keeps all but the soundest sleepers awake. (Temp H 33/90 L 22/71, Wind — 0–5 mph.)
21–40	Heavy rain from unseen clouds pummel the ship and those on deck. Waves can be seen in the dark like great gray-green boulders smashing against the ship every minute. The clouds press on the ship, cloaking all details over 10 feet away. Wind crashes against the vessel and its sail, trying to tear it from its supports. All loose items on deck vie for attention from the crashing waves or the blustery wind. (Temp H 33/91 L 27/80, Wind — 60–65 mph. Characters moving on deck must succeed on a saving throw each round or be knocked prone and pushed 10 feet in a random direction. All exposed areas of the ship are lightly obscured.)
41–60	Seemingly in rhythm with the lapping waves, periodic rain drops in vast amounts, quickly soaking all surfaces and washing away loose items. Waves roll languidly, topping six feet in height but not steep enough to make more than an exaggerated rocking motion. A light wind blows, carrying mist from the still warm water, visible in the occasional moonlight. (Temp H 76/25 L 71/22, Wind — 5–10 mph. Vision is reduced to one-half from the mist and the darkness. Darkvision is unaffected. Characters moving on deck must make a saving throw or be knocked prone. All exposed areas of the ship are lightly obscured.)
61–80	A drizzle of rain, varying in strength continuously throughout the nighttime hours. All surfaces are thoroughly soaked and heavy with water. The warmth of the day rapidly disappears, replaced with the humidity of the still evaporating water around the ship. Waves are present but pose no real threat to the direction of the ship. The wind blows constantly, keeping the sails full but not pushing the limit of its capabilities. (Temp H 80/27 L 78/26, Wind — 12–18 mph.)
81–00	A constant rain falls from gray clouds overhead, keeping all within it thoroughly soaked. The wind propels the ship slowly, seemingly held back by the rain, over the large hillock-shaped waves. Occasional lightning flashes illuminate the depth of the rain, looking like iron bars for as far as the eye can see, peppering the water. (Temp H 79/27 L 71/22, Wind — 5–10 mph. All exposed areas of the ship are lightly obscured.)

DRY/DAY

01–20	The large sun dominates the sky but a swift breeze keeps the temperature to a more moderate level. Spray pulled up from the many waves, capped in white froth. The horizon is marked with a large bank of gray clouds, promising rain in the next day or two. (Temp H 90/33 L 75/24, Wind — 10–15 mph.)
21–40	Clouds run amok along the sky, occasionally blocking the sun and its warmth. The wind seemingly growls as it tears across the water at the ship. The sail quivers, trying to keep the wind from escaping. Waves rise up and crash against the hull of the ship, each impact like a bludgeon from nature itself. (Temp H 89/32 L 77/26, Wind — 45–50 mph. Characters moving on deck must make a saving throw each round or be knocked prone.)
41–60	A crystal clear sky magnifies the sun, directing its heat against the ship and her crew. The wind puffs slowly, not enough to extinguish a candle, let alone cool the flesh of those in the open. Waves move across the water like a herd, trying to carry the ship along in their wake, fighting the vessel should it try to turn away. The spray carries over the rail into the faces of those on deck, quickly drying to leave powdered salt. (Temp H 92/34 L 87/31, Wind — 0–5 mph.)
61–80	The thick clouds overhead threaten to release their burden but maintain their hold for now. The moderate wind moves both the ship and the clouds, lifting the waves to heights of 10 feet, launching the spray into the air. The ship rolls with the impacts as it tips down one wave and up another, the prow having difficulty cutting through the water. (Temp H 89/32 L 82/29, Wind — 10–12 mph.)

81–00	The sky is clear, dotted with numerous small unimposing puffs of cloud. A steady wind blows, determined to cart items away in its embrace. The sun, high overhead, seems a greater distance than usual given the lack of heat generated. Abundant waves run to the horizon, making up for size with numbers. The water is churned to a gray-green, and you can see only a few feet under the surface with any clarity, another indicator of the weak sun. (Temp H 79/27 L 77/26, Wind — 18–20 mph.)

DRY/NIGHT

01–20	Clear sky provides a view of the numerous constellations and guiding stars. Wind gusts from the North East create a flapping staccato to match the waves breaking on the hull of the ship. Whitecapped waves, visible in the moonlight, reach for the sailors on board, topping seven to eight feet. A slight mist can be felt in the wind; consequently, all surfaces are slick and shiny with moisture. (Temp H 80/27 L 79/27, Wind — 15–25 mph. Characters moving on deck must succeed on a saving throw each round or be knocked prone.)
21–40	Clouds of stone gray run from horizon to horizon, extinguishing the stars and moon from view. The absence of wind allows the sails and rigging to hang listless, like cloth in a shop window. The water is unmarked, calm for many miles around the ship, waves visible in the far distance. Pressure seems to build, raising the temperature over several hours to just above a comfortable level. (Temp H 78/26 L 75/24, Wind — 0–5 mph. Experienced sailors know a storm is coming. Reroll on Tropical rain/day chart in 1d4 hours for result.)
41–60	The cool of the night is identified by the daytime heat escaping the decking, misting the moisture collected through the daylight hours. Besides raising the humidity to an uncomfortable level, it also deadens the night sounds of the creaking riggings and lapping waves. Lone trenches of waves roll the ship as it moves through them like long strides of a great beast. Occasional clouds plunge the ship into darkness, allowing the moon and stars to peer through again in a few moments. (Temp H 90/33 L 78/26, Wind — 10–20 mph.)
61–80	Moon and gray clouds do battle overhead for dominance, sometimes plunging the world into darkness or a dim twilight. Numerous waves about the size of a man run the length of the water as far as the eye can see, all topped with a cone of greenish white froth. The rigging and sails have rivulets of collected water, which pools on the deck. Lines are heavy with water and deck boards are slick and shiny, sometimes reflecting the occasional starlight. (Temp H 78/26 L 75/24, Wind — 20–25 mph. Characters moving on deck must succeed on a saving throw each round or be knocked prone. All exposed areas of the ship are lightly obscured.)
81–00	Clear ebony night overhead provides astronomers and navigators a fine view of the stars and planets. A gentle wind blows from the West, flapping the sail and nettings. Small waves lap against the side of the boat like a heartbeat, reflections of the moon on the waves stand out against the black background of the water and night sky. (Temp H 79/27 L 75/24, Wind — 5–10 mph.)

TEMPERATE

RAIN/DAY

01–20	A gentle breeze blows, adding a slight chill to the damp air. Large drops patter along the deck, occasionally warmed by the sun and quickly evaporating. Gray white clouds fill the sky from horizon to horizon, predicting a constant rainfall. Waves are large in width but not in height, rocking the ship with the passage. (Temp H 70/22 L 54/13, Wind — 5–10 mph.)
21–40	Intense rain from ebony clouds pummel the ship and those unfortunate enough to be on deck. Waves like great gray-green boulders smashing against the ship every minute. The overhead clouds descend to a point where it seems the ship is in a large subterranean chamber. The sail struggles to remain attached to the mast as the wind tries to rip it from the rigging. All loose items on deck vie for attention from the crashing waves or the blustery wind. (Temp H 64/18 L 62/17, Wind — 70–75 mph. Characters moving on deck must make a saving throw each round or be knocked prone and pushed 10 feet in a random direction. All exposed areas of the ship are lightly obscured.)
41–60	The sky carries a darker shade than normal, clouds so thick they block out all trace of light. Rain is propelled horizontally with the wind, hitting like daggers and needles, reducing vision to mere feet around each person. Winds blow loose objects and people unprepared for its force off course. Waves 15–30 feet high assault the ship, blowing over the rail and soaking sailors with its frigid embrace. (Temp H 79/27 L 75/24, Wind — 27–35 mph. Characters moving on deck must succeed on a saving throw or be knocked prone and pushed 10 feet in a random direction. All exposed areas of the ship are heavily obscured.)
61–80	A constant rain falls from gray clouds overhead, keeping all within it thoroughly soaked. The wind propels the ship slowly, seemingly held back by the rain, over the large hillock-shaped waves. Occasional lightning flashes illuminate the depth of the rain, looking like iron bars for as far as the eye can see, peppering the water. (Temp H 61/17 L 53/12, Wind — 5–10 mph. All exposed areas of the ship are lightly obscured.)
81–00	A simple rain falls, creating a constant drone of rain on the wooden deck. The wind is not strong enough to alter the vertical direction of the rain, letting the sail hang like a soaked rag from the mast. The subtle waves rock the ship almost undetectably as they move on under currents. Clouds looking like an inverted mountain range press down upon the ship and crew. (Temp H 48/9 L 44/2, Wind — 5–20 mph.)

RAIN/NIGHT

01–20	Lightning-rippled clouds streak by overhead, waves lift like cliffs (six to 15 feet) around the vessel. Rain alternates from side to side and straight down with the force of a hammer blow. Rivers of water course around the deck from the rain and waves, creating treacherous footing for all on board. The sails snap and crack as it fills with the wind, dropping deluges of collected rain to the deck below. Periodically, the sky lights up with a lightning blast nearby, painting everything in shades of white and gray; all other times, the charcoal sky and water bestow a sense of isolation. (Temp H 37/3 L 36/2, Wind — 55–60 mph. Characters moving on deck must succeed on a saving throw with a –1 penalty each round or be knocked prone and pushed 15 feet in a random direction. All exposed areas of the ship are lightly obscured.)
21–40	A constant rain falls from gray clouds overhead, keeping all within it thoroughly soaked. The wind propels the ship slowly, seemingly held back by the rain, over the large hillock-shaped waves. Occasional lightning flashes illuminate the depth of the rain, looking like iron bars for as far as the eye can see, peppering the water. (Temp H 42/6 L 39/5, Wind — 5–10 mph NE-E. All exposed areas of the ship are lightly obscured.)

41–60
Thick rolling clouds erupt constantly with thunder and rain beating upon the wooden planks. The percussion of the rain is accented with the occasional spray of mountainous waves carried on the wind. Gusts of wind blow across the ship, attempting to pull everything along in its wake. Sight is reduced to feet, distance eliminated with the thick sheets of rain. (Temp H 59/16 L 48/10, Wind — 15–20 mph. Characters moving on deck must succeed on a saving throw each round or be knocked prone. All exposed areas of the ship are heavily obscured.)

61–80
Hurricane force rain and wind, the ship is tossed like a child's doll. Huge waves like mountains threaten to topple the vessel and launch the sailors into the unforgiving sea. Wind blows fiercely lifting all heavy objects not lashed down and propelling them around and off the ship. The sky and water are distinguishable, erasing the horizon as both are steel gray. (Temp H 62/17 L 54/13, Wind — 60–80 mph. Characters on deck must succeed on a saving throw with a –2 penalty each round or be knocked prone and pushed 20 feet in a random direction. All exposed areas of the ship are heavily obscured.)

81–00
A simple rain falls, creating a constant drone of rain on the wooden deck. The wind is not strong enough to alter the vertical direction of the rain, letting the sail hang like a soaked rag from the mast. The subtle waves rock the ship almost undetectably as they move on under currents. Clouds looking like an inverted mountain range press down upon the ship and crew. Navigation can only be done through compass or landmarks. (Temp H 59/16 L 58/15, Wind — 5–10 mph.)

DRY/DAY

01–20
The large sun dominates the sky, but a swift breeze keeps the temperature to a cooler level. Spray pulled up from the many waves, capped in white froth and thrown across the deck. The horizon is marked with a large bank of gray clouds, promising rain in the next day or two. (Temp H 48/10 L 35/2, Wind — 10–15 mph.)

21–40
The sky is clear, dotted with numerous small unimposing puffs of cloud. A steady wind blows determined to cart items away in its embrace. The sun, high overhead seems a greater distance than usual given the lack of heat generated. Abundant waves run to the horizon, making up for size with numbers. The water is churned to a gray-green, and you can see only a few feet under the surface with any clarity, another indicator of the weak sun. (Temp H 70/22 L 54/13, Wind — 18–20 mph.)

41–60
A crystal clear sky magnifies the sun directing its heat against the ship and her crew. The wind puffs slowly, not enough to extinguish a candle let alone cool the flesh of those warmer than usual day. Waves move across the water like a herd, trying to carry the ship along in their wake, fighting the vessel should it try to turn away. The spray carries over the rail into the faces of those on deck, quickly drying to leave traces of powdered salt. (Temp H 82/29 L 68/21, Wind — 5–10 mph. Sunstroke in 3d8 rounds unless properly attired for the sun.)

61–80
Sun and gray clouds do battle overhead for dominance, sometimes plunging the water into a dark twilight or bright daylight. Numerous waves, about the size of a man run the length of the water as far as the eye can see, all topped with a cone of white froth. The wind picks this froth from each and carries it along and coats all surfaces. This cooling spray makes the trip enjoyable for most on board, even in the shade. The rigging and sails flap in the breeze, occasionally dropping additional sprays to the deck, glinting like jewels in the periodic sun. (Temp H 75/25 L 61/17, Wind — 18–20 mph.)

81–00
Gray the color of stone has been painted from horizon to horizon, plunging the day into twilight. The absence of wind allows the sails and rigging to hang listless, like cloth in a shop window. The water is unmarked, calm for many miles around the ship, waves visible in the far distance. Pressure seems to build, raising the temperature over several hours to a more comfortable level. (Temp H 64/18 L 51/11, Wind — 5–10 mph. Reroll in four game hours on the wet-day chart for the approaching storm.)

DRY/NIGHT

01–20
Clear sky provides a view of the numerous constellations and guiding stars. Wind gusts from the North East creating a flapping staccato to match the waves breaking on the hull of the ship. Whitecapped waves, visible in the moonlight,, reach for the sailors on board, topping seven to eight feet. A slight mist can be felt in the wind; consequently, all surfaces are slick and shiny with moisture (Temp G 39/5 L 37/3, Wind — 15–25 mph. Characters moving on deck must succeed on a saving throw each round or be knocked prone.)

21–40
Clear ebony night overhead provides astronomers and navigators a fine view of the stars and planets. A gentle wind blows from the South flapping the sail and nettings. Small waves lap against the side of the boat like a heartbeat; small whitecaps stand out stark against the black background of the water and night sky. (Temp H 64/18 L 62/17, Wind — 15–25 mph.)

41–60
An overcast sky blocks the view of all but the brightest stars and planets. Some navigation can still be done by experienced sailors. A breeze comes and goes, proving to be a fickle asset for the sails on the ship, waves playing tag gently rock the ship back and forth. (Temp H 79/27 L 75/24, Wind — 5–10 mph.)

61–80
Numerous stars turn the night sky into a twilight gray, offsetting the jet black of the calm water. A steady soft wind blows propelling the ship along on its way. The sound of the surf being cut by the hull is seemingly alone, periodically joined by the creak of the rigging and the soft voice of a sailor. (Temp H 61/17 L 53/12, Wind — 10–15 mph.)

81–00
A severe wind blows, threatening to rip the sail from the mast, and propels the vessel over the waves like a toy. Thick ribbons of cloud race overhead like gray gashes in the constellations. Many large waves run the length of vision, occasionally growing to such a large size (45 feet) that they threaten to topple the ship like flotsam. (Temp H 48/9 L 44/2, Wind — 60–65 mph. Characters on deck must succeed on a saving throw to move about at more than half speed.)

ARCTIC

Wind chill is a real concern when the temperature drops below 32° F. Exposure to the wind risks frostbite for flesh. The effective temperature, for purposes of calculating potential harm caused by extreme cold, can be found in the Wind Chill Table.

RAIN/DAY

01–20
White gray clouds span from horizon to horizon, periodic deluges of snow drop upon the water and ship. The deck is quickly covered in a white blanket of snow, making progress slow around the ship. Finding equipment is difficult for the inexperienced sailor, boxes and barrels becoming nondescript objects in the snow. The wind moves the snow in various directions as it descends, moving the sails to half full with their strongest force. (Temp H –10/–23 L –15/–26, Wind — 10–15 mph. See rules above for the consequences of exposure to extreme temperatures.)

21–40	Sleet drops like sheets of needles upon sailors in the open. The wind drives the sleet almost horizontally across the waves. Large mountains of water move across the area threatening to bash the vessel into submission. The steel gray sky rolls like the underside of a surf promising many hours of attack. The rigging creaks and sails moan ominously in the barrage of the storm. Movement along the deck is perilous at best; those in the upper reaches of the vessel cling for their lives. (Temp H –15/–27 L –25/–31, Wind — 20–25 mph. See rules above for the consequences of exposure to extreme temperatures. Characters moving on deck must succeed a saving throw each round or be knocked prone and be pushed 10 feet in a random direction. All exposed areas of the ship are lightly obscured.)
41–60	Freezing mist falls like a cloud landing on water. Wind is present but too weak to fill sails. Ice floes move on the sunken currents, dancing around the ship at great distances. Waves are subdued, seemingly moving in numerous directions, with no discernible pattern. Ice forms on most surfaces with extended exposure, and sails and rigging becoming rigid and hazardous with each passing hour. (Temp H –15/–26 L –20/–29, Wind — 0–5 mph. See rules above for the consequences of exposure to extreme temperatures. Characters moving on deck must succeed on a saving throw each round or be knocked prone. All exposed areas of the ship are lightly obscured.)
61–80	Lightning-rippled clouds streak by overhead, waves lift like cliffs (six to 15 feet) around the vessel. Rain and sleet alternate from side to side and straight down with the force of a hammer blow. Ice coats all exposed surfaces in minutes, creating treacherous areas on the ship and rigging. The sails snap and crack as it fills with the wind, snow, and ice, chunks of collected ice dropping ice dropping to the deck below. Periodically, the sky lights up with a lightning blast nearby painting everything with in shades of white and gray, all other times the charcoal sky and water bestow a sense of isolation. (Temp H –20/–29 L –31/–35, Wind — 25–35 mph N. All exposed areas of the ship are lightly obscured. There is a 10% chance of course change being required for ice formation in path of ship. See rules above for the consequences of exposure to extreme temperatures.)
81–00	The sky carries a darker shade than normal, clouds so thick they block out all trace of light. Rain is propelled horizontally with the wind, hitting like daggers and needles, and reducing vision to mere feet around each person. Ice forms on all surfaces, making passage difficult on deck. Winds blow loose objects and people unprepared for its force off course. Waves five to 30 feet high assault the ship, blowing over the rail and soaking sailors with its frigid embrace. (Temp H –20/–29 L –29/–34 mph. See rules above for the consequences of exposure to extreme temperatures. Characters moving on deck must succeed on a saving throw each round or be knocked prone and pushed 10 feet in a random direction. All exposed areas of the ship are heavily obscured.)

Rain/Night

Rain/ Day	Lightning-rippled clouds streak by overhead, and waves lift like cliffs (six to 15 feet) around the vessel. Hail alternates from side-to-side and straight down with the force of a hammer blow. Ice coats all exposed surfaces in minutes, creating treacherous areas on the ship and rigging. The sails snap and crack as it fills with the wind, snow, and ice, dropping chunks of ice to the deck below. Periodically, the sky lights up with a nearby lightning blast that paints everything within shades of white and gray; all other times, the charcoal sky and water bestow a sense of isolation. (Temp H –20/–29 L –31/–35, Wind — 45–50 mph. Characters moving on deck must succeed on a saving throw or be knocked prone and pushed 10 feet in a random direction. All exposed areas of the ship are heavily obscured. See rules above for the consequences of exposure to extreme temperatures.)

21–40	Freezing mist falls like a cloud landing on the water. Wind is present but too weak to fill sails. Ice floes move on the sunken currents, dancing around the ship at great distances. Waves are subdued, seemingly moving in numerous directions, no pattern discernible. Ice forms on most surfaces with extended exposure, sails and rigging becoming rigid and hazardous with each passing hour. (Temp H –15/–23 L –20/–29, Wind — 0–5 mph. Characters moving on deck must succeed on a saving throw each round or be knocked prone. All exposed areas of the ship are lightly obscured. See rules above for the consequences of exposure to extreme temperatures.)
41–60	The night sky carries a darker shade than normal, clouds so thick they block out all trace of light. Rain is propelled horizontally with the wind, hitting like daggers and needles, and reducing vision to mere feet around each person. Ice forms on all surfaces making passage difficult on deck. Winds blow loose objects and people unprepared for its force off course. Waves 15–30 feet high assault the ship, blowing over the rail and soaking sailors with its frigid embrace. (Temp H –20/–29 L –29/–34, Wind — 27–35 mph. Characters moving on deck must succeed on a saving throw each round or be knocked prone and pushed 10 feet in a random direction. All exposed areas of the ship are lightly obscured. See rules above for the consequences of exposure to extreme temperatures.)
61–80	Constant icy drizzle settles on all surfaces, turning the dark night into a dark gray, reducing vision to nearly non-existent. Frigid temperatures freeze the moisture within minutes on every surface. Travel across deck is difficult but manageable to those familiar with surroundings. Sound is subdued with the ice pellets, adding a muffling effect to conversations. Waves are unseen but can be felt hitting the deck every few seconds, occasionally bathing the deck with its spray, a testament to their height of several feet. (Temp H –10/–23 L –15/–26, Wind — 5–10 mph. Characters moving on deck must succeed on a saving throw each round or be knocked prone. All exposed areas of the ship are lightly obscured.)
81–00	Large thick flakes drop around the ship, landing softly on the water before melting. Equipment and decking are quickly covered in a thick blanket of white snow. Waves roll languidly, topping six feet in height but not steep enough to make more than an exaggerated rocking motion. A light wind blows carrying the flakes on the air currents, visible in the occasional moonlight. (Temp H 19/–7 L –2/–19, Wind — 5–10 mph. Characters moving on deck must succeed on a saving throw each round or be knocked prone. All exposed areas of the ship are lightly obscured.)

Dry/Day

01–20	Clear blue sky overhead provides ample room for the bright sun to shine. Wind gusts from the northeast, flapping the sail and nettings. Whitecapped waves, topping seven to eight feet high, seem to push large chunks of ice along in their grasp. (Temp H –21/–29 L –28/–33, Wind — 10–15 mph. Those working while facing the sun must succeed on a saving throw or be blinded for 1d4 hours. Characters with a natural sensitivity to light take a –1 penalty on this saving throw. There is a 10% chance of a course changed being required for ice floe in the path of ship.)
21–40	Sun and gray clouds do battle overhead for dominance, sometimes plunging the water into a dark twilight or bright daylight. Numerous waves about the size of a man run the length of the water as far as the eye can see, all topped with a cone of white froth. The wind picks this froth from each and carries it along, freezing it to any surface it covers. The rigging and sails labor under the extra weight of the ice, glinting like jewels in the periodic sun. (Temp H –25/–32 L –32/–36, Wind — 20–25 mph. Characters moving on deck must succeed on a saving throw each round or be knocked prone. There is a 12% chance of a course change being required for ice floe in the path of ship.)

41–60	Gray, the color of stone, has been painted from horizon to horizon, plunging the day into twilight. The absence of wind allows the sails and rigging to hang listless, like cloth in a shop window. The water is unmarked, calm for many miles around the ship, with waves visible in the far distance. Pressure seems to build, raising the temperature over several hours to a more comfortable level. Icebergs in the distance hold steady like islands. (Temp H –17/–27 L –20/–29, Wind — 0–5 mph. Experienced sailors know a storm is coming. Reroll on Arctic day-rain chart in 1d4 hours for result. There is a 2% chance of a course change being required for icebergs in the path of ship.)
61–80	Streamers of billowy clouds race overhead in the wind. Large waves buffet the ship and attempt to carry it along with them. Wind assaults the vessel hard from the west, never wavering or letting up. Tacking into the wind seems impossible from its vicious force while tacking with the wind runs a risk of never getting control of the ship back. (Temp H –20/–29 L –27/–33, Wind — 35–40 mph. Characters moving on deck must succeed on a saving throw each round or be knocked prone and pushed five feet in a random direction.)
81–00	The air burns with the wind chill, crusting ice all over the ship, the sun adding no aid to the frigid temperature. Clouds are nonexistent in the sky, collecting only on the horizons. While filling the sails, the wind steals the breath from those on deck and freezes exposed flesh in minutes. (Temp H –18/–28 L –35/–37, Wind — 45–50 mph. Characters moving on deck must succeed on a saving throw each round or be knocked prone and pushed 10 feet in a random direction.)

Dry/Night

01–20	Clear ebony night overhead provides astronomers and navigators a fine view of the stars and planets. A gentle wind blows from the south, flapping the sail and nettings. Small waves lap against the side of the boat like a heartbeat, icebergs stand out stark white against the black background of the water and night sky. (Temp H –20/–29 L –25/–32, Wind — 5–10 mph. There is a 10% chance of a course change being required for an ice floe in path of ship.)
21–40	Large clouds move overhead, blocking the stars and moon with their bulk. The ship rolls gently on the waves as it rides through the water. Occasionally, larger waves provide a small drop for the vessel as it is carried over the lip of the wave. The strong wind takes the ship along with it, filling the sails and pulling at cloaks of those on board. (Temp H –22/–30 L –26/–32, Wind — 10–15 mph.)
41–60	Clouds block all stars and only hint at the location of the moon, adding a claustrophobic feel to the trip. The absence of wind allows the sails and rigging to hang listless, like cloth in a shop window. The ebony water ripples in the soft breeze, whitecaps standing out like glowing embers. (Temp H –19/–28 L –25/–32, Wind — 0–5 mph. There is a 2% chance of a course change being required for icebergs in the path of ship.)
61–80	Partial clouds cover sections of the sky, seemingly unmoving. Large waves buffet the ship and attempt to carry it along with them. Wind assaults the vessel hard from the west, never wavering or letting up. Travel during the night at full sail run double risk of colliding with ice. (Temp H –25/–31 L –29/–33, Wind — 25–35 mph. Characters moving on deck must succeed on a saving throw each round or be knocked prone. There is a 15% chance of a course change for ice.)
80–00	Wisps of cloud move across the sky sometimes blocking the stars. The brightness of the visible stars and moon provides ample light to maneuver around the ship and perform most tasks. The ever-present wind provides enough force to keep the ship moving at optimum speed. The absence of spray from the calm waters allows for equipment to dry. (Temp H –29/–34 L –31/–35, Wind — 20–25 mph.)

Equatorial

Within the Equatorial region, humidity is an issue for temperature measurement. Reference to the Humidity Table will bring about a more realistic gauge for temperature; consequently, the effects of heat upon those traveling the waves should be watched closely.

Rain/Day

01–20	A heavy wind blows, adding a texture to the warm rain falling. Large drops patter along the deck, occasional sunshine warms the decks and quickly evaporates the rain and adds to the humidity. A sticky aspect of the air grows throughout the day as the humidity rises. Sunlight glints off the water like numerous smaller suns, blinding those not ready for the effect. Waves are large in width but not in height, rocking the ship with their passage. (Temp H 89/32 L 80/27, Wind — 30–35 mph.)
21–40	Heavy rain pummels the ship and those on board, quickly soaking all equipment and people. The waves are sedate, rarely topping five feet, seemingly held down with the impact of the rain. The sun tries to pierce the cloud cover with its intense glare, but only succeeds in raising the temperature. Wind is nonexistent, hammered to submission by the heavy rain. (Temp H 75/24 L 71/22, Wind — 0–5 mph.)
41–60	Seemingly in rhythm with the lapping waves, periodic rain drops in vast amounts, quickly soaking all surfaces and washing away loose items. Between rainfalls, the sun attempts to burn away the moisture with blistering heat, never quite successfully, and so leaves all with a heaviness of moisture. Waves roll languidly topping six feet in height but are not steep enough to make more than an exaggerated rocking motion. The wind blows merrily, billowing out the sails of the ship and propelling the vessel over the large waves. (Temp H 79/27 L 71/22, Wind — 10–15 mph. Characters moving on deck during a deluge must succeed on a saving throw or be knocked prone and pushed 10 feet in a random direction.)
61–80	A drizzle of rain, sometimes hard and sometimes light, falls continuously throughout the day. All surfaces are thoroughly soaked and heavy with water. The warmth of the occasional sun is diminished slightly by the cool rain, keeping it tolerable for all involved. Waves are present but pose little threat to the navigation of the ship or to the course she desires to take. The wind blows constantly, keeping the sails full but not pushing the limit of its capabilities. (Temp H 87/31 L 78/26, Wind — 15–20 mph.)
81–00	Heavy rain from unseen clouds pummels the ship and those on deck. Waves like great gray-green boulders smash against the ship every minute. The overhead clouds descend to a point where it seems the ship is in a large chamber. Wind hurtles against the vessel and its sail, trying to rip it free from the mast and rigging. All loose items are tossed around the decking, creating hazards for those on deck. (Temp H 80/27 L 74/24, Wind — 50–55 mph. Characters moving on deck must succeed on a saving throw each round or be knocked prone and pushed 10 feet in a random direction.)

Rain/Night

01–20	The humidity of the night is made comfortable by the patter of rain upon the deck. The coolness of the rain seems to steal some of the weight of the air. The thin clouds mask the presence of the stars but leave a large halo where the moon tries to shine. The waves crash against the hull as if trying to keep the ship from reaching its goal. The bounce of the ship as it passes over the waves keeps all but the soundest sleepers awake. (Temp H 80/27 L 71/22, Wind — 0–5 mph.)

21–40 Heavy rain from ebony clouds presses down on the ship and those on deck. Waves can be seen in the dark like great gray-green boulders that smash against the ship every minute. The overhead clouds descend to a point where it seems the ship is in a large chamber. Wind hurtles against the vessel and its sail, trying to rip it from the mast and rigging. All loose items on deck vie for attention from the crashing waves or the blustery wind. (Temp H 77/26 L 62/17, Wind — 20–25 mph. Characters moving on deck must succeed on a saving throw each round or be knocked prone. All exposed areas of the ship are lightly obscured.)

41–60 Seemingly in rhythm with the lapping waves, periodic rain drops in vast amounts, quickly soaking all surfaces and washing away loose materials. Waves roll languidly, topping six feet in height but not steep enough to make more than an exaggerated rocking motion. A light wind blows, carrying a humid mist from the still warm water, visible in the intermittent moonlight. (Temp H 76/25 L 71/22, Wind — 5–10 mph. Characters moving on deck must succeed on a saving throw each round or be knocked prone and pushed 10 feet in a random direction. All exposed areas of the ship are lightly obscured.)

61–80 A drizzle of rain, sometimes hard and sometimes light, falls continuously during the nighttime hours. All surfaces are thoroughly soaked and heavy with water. The warmth of the day rapidly disappears, replaced with the humidity of the still-evaporating water around the ship. The waves are smaller than normal and work with the rain to stay weak enough to be inconsequential. The wind blows constantly, keeping the sails full but not pushing the limit of its capabilities. (Temp H 80/27 L 78/26, Wind — 12–18 mph.)

81–00 A thrashing rain accompanies hurricane force winds. In the distance amid lightning flashes, waterspouts can be seen reaching for the sky. Waves the size of small mountains rise above the vessel, giving the ship a wide span of view when atop a wave and a sense of claustrophobia when in a gully. (Temp H 79/27 L 71/22, Wind — 45–50 mph. Characters moving on deck must succeed on a saving throw with a −1 penalty each round or be knocked prone and pushed 15 feet in a random direction. All exposed areas of the ship are lightly obscured.)

Dry/Day

01–20 The large sun dominates the sky but a swift breeze keeps the temperature to a more moderate level. Spray pulled up from the many waves is capped in white froth. The horizon is marked with a large bank of gray clouds that promise rain in the next day or two. The humidity rises throughout the day and adds a weight to the sun that saps the strength of those not acquainted with the equatorial waters. (Temp H 81/28 L 75/24, Wind — 10–15 mph.)

21–40 Clouds run amok along the sky, occasionally blocking the sun and its warmth. The wind seemingly growls as it tears across the water at the ship. The sail quivers, trying to keep the wind from escaping. Waves rise up and crash against the hull of the ship, each impact like a bludgeon from nature itself. (Temp H 77/26 L 74/24, Wind — 60–65 mph. Characters moving on deck must succeed on a saving throw each round or be knocked prone and pushed 10 feet in a random direction.)

41–60 A crystal-clear sky magnifies the sun, directing its heat against the ship and her crew. The wind puffs slowly, not enough to extinguish a candle, let alone cool the flesh of those in the open. Waves move across the water like a herd, trying to carry the ship along in their wake, fighting the vessel should it try to turn away. The spray carries over the rail into the faces of those on deck, quickly drying to leave powdered salt. (Temp H 77/26 L 74/23, Wind — 0–5 mph.)

61–80 The thick clouds overhead threaten to release their burden, moisture released in the form of a thick palpable air. While no rain has fallen during the day, all surfaces are beaded with sweat and spray from the moisture-laced air. The moderate wind moves the ship and the clouds, lifting the waves to heights of 10 feet and launching the spray into the air. The ship rolls with the impacts as it tips down one wave and up another, the prow having difficulty cutting through the water. (Temp H 77/26 L 75/24, Wind — 10–12 mph.)

81–00 The sky is clear and dotted with numerous small, unimposing puffs of cloud. A steady wind blows, determined to cart items away in its embrace. The sun, high overhead, seems at a greater distance than usual given the lack of heat generated. Abundant waves run to the horizon, making up for size with numbers. The water is churned to a gray-green, and you can see only a few feet under the surface with any clarity, another indicator of the weak sun. (Temp H 79/27 L 77/26, Wind — 20–25 mph.)

Dry/Night

01–20 Clear sky provides a view of the numerous constellations and guiding stars. Wind gusts from the southwest, creating a flapping staccato to match the waves breaking on the hull of the ship. Whitecapped waves, visible in the moonlight, reach for the sailors on board, topping seven to eight feet. A slight mist can be felt in the wind; consequently, all surfaces are slick and shiny with moisture. (Temp H 75/25 L 61/17, Wind — 15–25 mph. Characters moving on deck must succeed on a saving throw each round or be knocked prone.)

21–40 Clouds of stone gray run from horizon to horizon, extinguishing the stars and moon from view. The absence of wind allows the sails and rigging to hang listless, like cloth in a shop window. The water is unmarked, calm for many miles around the ship, waves visible in the far distance. Pressure seems to build, raising the temperature over several hours to just above a comfortable level. (Temp H 76/25 L 75/24, Wind — 0–5 mph. Experienced sailors know a storm is coming. Reroll on Equatorial day–rain chart in 1d4 hours for result.)

41–60 The cool of the night is identified by the daytime heat escaping the decking, misting the moisture collected through the daylight hours. Besides raising the humidity to an uncomfortable level, it also deadens the night sounds of the creaking riggings and lapping waves. Long trenches of waves roll the ship as it moves through them like long strides of a great beast. Occasional clouds plunge the ship into darkness, allowing the moon and stars to peer through again in a few moments. (Temp H 76/25 L 69/21, Wind — 10–20 mph.)

61–80 Periodic clouds block the moon and stars, stealing their dim light and guidance. Numerous waves about the size of a man run the length of the water as far as the eye can see, all topped with a cone of greenish-white froth. The rigging and sails have rivulets of collected water that pools on the deck. Lines are heavy with water, and deck boards are slick and shiny, reflecting any light source. (Temp H 78/26 L 75/24, Wind — 20–25 mph. Characters moving on deck must succeed on a saving throw each round or be knocked prone.)

81–00 Clear ebony night overhead provides astronomers and navigators a fine view of the stars and planets. A gentle wind blows from the west, flapping the sail and nettings. Small waves lap against the side of the boat like a heartbeat, and reflections of the moon on the waves stand out stark white against the black background of the water and night sky. (Temp H 79/27 L 75/24, Wind — 5–10 mph.)

Spring

Tropical

Heatstroke is a risk for any who travel the warm regions of the world. Those exerting themselves must succeed on a saving throw for each hour of strenuous work or become exhausted (–1 to hit, damage and saves). For each cumulative hour of strenuous work, the save is made with a cumulative –1 penalty. Resting in shaded areas for 10 minutes per hour negates the –1 penalty for that hour. Spell components run a 10% chance of spoiling in humidity, if you determine they are subject to such damage.

Rain/Day

01–20	A gentle breeze blows, adding a pleasant cooling to the warm rain falling. Large drops patter along the deck, and occasional sunshine warms the deck, quickly evaporating the rain and adding to the humidity. A sticky aspect of the air grows throughout the day as the humidity rises. Sunlight sparkles off the water like numerous smaller suns, blinding those unprepared for the effect. Waves are large in width but not in height, rocking the ship with their passage. (Temp H 85/30 L 78/26, Wind — 5–10 mph.)
21–40	Heavy rain pummels the ship and those on board, quickly drenching all equipment and people. The waves are minimal, rarely topping five feet, seemingly held down with the rain. The sun tries to penetrate the cloud cover with its intense glare, but only succeeds in raising the temperature. Wind is nonexistent, hammered to submission by the heavy rain. (Temp H 91/33 L 88/31, Wind — 0–5 mph.)
41–60	Seemingly in rhythm with the lapping waves, periodic rain drops in vast amounts, quickly soaking all surfaces and washing away loose items. Between rainfalls, the sun attempts to burn away the moisture with blistering heat. Waves roll languidly, topping six feet in height but not steep enough to make more than an exaggerated rocking motion. The wind blows merrily, billowing out the sails of the ship and propelling the vessel over the large waves. (Temp H 89/32 L 71/22, Wind — 10–15 mph. Characters moving on deck during a deluge must succeed on a saving throw or be knocked prone and pushed 10 feet in a random direction.)
61–80	A drizzle of rain, alternating between light and hard, falls continuously throughout the day. All surfaces are thoroughly waterlogged and heavy with water. The warmth of the occasional sun is diminished slightly by the cool rain, keeping it tolerable for all involved. Waves are present but pose no real threat to the direction of the ship or her course. The wind blows constantly and keeps the sails full but doesn't push the limit of its capabilities. (Temp H 86/30 L 75/24, Wind — 30–35 mph.)
81–00	Grayish clouds dump heavy rains upon the ship and her riders. Waves like great gray-green boulders smash against the ship every minute. The overhead clouds descend to a point where it seems the ship is in a large chamber. Wind hurtles against the vessel and its sail, trying to rip it from the mast and rigging. All loose items on deck vie for attention from the crashing waves or the blustery wind. (Temp H 90/33 L 80/27, Wind — 20–25 mph. Characters moving on deck must succeed on a saving throw each round or be knocked prone. All exposed areas of the ship are lightly obscured.)

Rain/Night

01–20	The cool of the night is accompanied by the patter of rain upon the deck. The humidity keeps the coolness of the night from becoming comfortable. The moon makes itself known through the clouds, illuminating a portion of the night sky to milky white. The waves crash against the hull as if trying to keep the ship from reaching its goal. The bounce of the ship as it passes over the waves keeps all but the soundest sleepers awake. (Temp H 89/32 L 78/26, Winds — 0–15 mph.)
21–40	Falling rain eliminates possible viewing of any distance greater than 50 feet. Waves can be seen in the dark like great gray-green boulders and smash against the ship every minute. Wind hurtles against the vessel and its sail, trying to rip it from the mast and rigging. The strong wind tries to steal any small items from the ship through sheer determination and strength. (Temp H 87/31 L 81/27, Wind — 45–50 mph. Characters moving on deck must succeed on a saving throw each round or be knocked prone and pushed 10 feet in a random direction. All exposed areas of the ship are lightly obscured.)
41–60	The waves rock the ship in cadence to the heavy rain, quickly soaking all surfaces and washing away loose items. Waves roll languidly, topping six feet in height but are not steep enough to make more than an exaggerated rolling motion. A light wind blows and carries mist from the still warm water, visible in the occasional moonlight. (Temp H 85/30 L 78/26, Wind — 5–10 mph. Characters moving on deck during a deluge must succeed on a saving throw each round or be knocked prone and pushed 10 feet in a random direction. All exposed areas of the ship are lightly obscured.)
61–80	A thick misting of rain keeps all items and equipment saturated. The comfort of the day rapidly disappears, replaced with the humidity of the still-evaporating water around the ship. Waves are present but pose no real threat to the ship. The wind blows constantly, keeping the sails full but not pushing the limit of its capabilities. (Temp H 83/28 L 72/222, Wind — 25–30 mph.)
81–00	A continual rain falls from gray clouds overhead, keeping all within it thoroughly soaked. The wind propels the ship slowly, seemingly held back by the rain, over the large hillock-shaped waves. Occasional lightning flashes illuminate the depth of the rain, looking like iron bars for as far as the eye can see, peppering the water. (Temp H 89/32 L 85/30, Wind — 5–10 mph. All exposed areas of the ship are lightly obscured.)

Dry/Day

01–20	The large sun dominates the sky but a swift breeze keeps the temperature to a more moderate level. Spray is pulled up from the many waves, capped in white froth. The horizon is marked with a large bank of gray clouds promising rain in the next day or two. (Temp H 91/33 L 79/26, Wind — 20–25 mph.)
21–40	Clouds run amok along the sky, occasionally blocking the sun and its warmth. The wind seemingly howls as it tears across the water at the ship. The sail quivers, trying to keep the wind from escaping. Waves rise up and crash against the hull of the ship, each impact like a bludgeon from nature itself. (Temp H 86/30 L 79/26, Wind — 60–65 mph. Characters moving on deck must succeed on a saving throw each round or be knocked prone and pushed 10 feet in a random direction.)
41–60	A crystal-clear sky magnifies the sun, directing its heat against the ship and her crew. The wind puffs slowly, not enough to quench the heat from the flesh of those in the open. Waves move across the water like a herd, trying to carry the ship along in their wake, fighting the vessel should it try to turn away. The spray carries over the rail into the faces of those on deck, quickly drying to leave powdered salt. (Temp H 85/30 L 73/23, Wind — 0–5 mph.)

61–80	The thick clouds overhead threaten to release their burden but maintain their hold for now. The moderate wind moves both the ship and the clouds, lifting the waves to heights of 10 feet, launching the spray into the air. The ship rolls with the impacts as it tips down one wave and up another, the prow having difficulty cutting through the water. (Temp H 87/31 L 79/26, Wind — 20–25 mph.)
81–00	The sky is clear, dotted with numerous small, unimposing puffs of cloud. A steady wind blows, determined to cart items away in its embrace. The sun, high overhead, seems at a greater distance than usual given the lack of heat generated. Abundant waves run to the horizon, making up for size with numbers. The water is churned to a gray-green, and you can see only a few feet under the surface with any clarity, another indicator of the weak sun. (Temp H 84/29 L 72/22, Wind — 18–20 mph.)

Dry/Night

01–20	Clear sky provides a view of the numerous constellations and guiding stars. Wind gusts from the northeast, creating a flapping staccato to match the waves breaking on the hull of the ship. Whitecapped waves, visible in the moonlight, reach for the sailors on board, topping seven to eight feet. A slight mist can be felt in the wind; consequently, all surfaces are slick and shiny with moisture. (Temp H 86/30 L 75/24, Wind — 15–25 mph. Characters moving on deck must succeed on a saving throw each round or be knocked prone.)
21–40	Clouds of stone gray run from horizon to horizon, extinguishing the stars and moon from view. The absence of wind allows the sails and rigging to hang listless, like cloth in a shop window. The water is unmarked, calm for many miles around the ship, with waves visible in the far distance. Pressure seems to build, raising the temperature over several hours to just above a comfortable level. (Temp H 78/26 L 73/23, Wind — 0–5 mph. Experienced sailors know a storm is coming. Reroll on Tropical day–rain chart in 1d4 hours for result.)
41–60	The cool of the night is easily identified by the daytime heat escaping the decking, misting the moisture collected through the daylight hours. Besides raising the humidity to an uncomfortable level, it also deadens the night sounds of the creaking riggings and lapping waves. Long trenches of waves roll the ship as it moves through them like long strides of a great beast. Occasional clouds plunge the ship into darkness, allowing the moon and stars to peer through again in a few moments. (Temp H 88/31 L 80/27, Wind — 10–20 mph.)
61–80	Moon and gray clouds do battle overhead for dominance, sometimes plunging the world into a dark twilight or bright daylight. Numerous waves about the size of a man run the length of the water as far as the eye can see, all topped with a cone of grayish white froth. The rigging and sails have rivulets of collected water, which pools on the deck. Lines are heavy with water, and deck boards are slick and shiny, sometimes reflecting the occasional illumination. (Temp H 78/26 L 75/24, Wind — 20–25 mph. Characters moving on deck must succeed on a saving throw each round or be knocked prone.)
81–00	Clear ebony night overhead provides astronomers and navigators a fine view of the stars and planets. A gentle wind blows from the west, flapping the sail and nettings. Small waves lap against the side of the boat like a heartbeat, reflections of the moon on the waves stand out stark white against the black background of the water and night sky. (Temp H 75/24 L 72/22, Wind — 5–10 mph.)

Temperate

Rain/Day

01–20	A gentle breeze blows, adding a slight chill to the damp air. Large drops patter along the deck, occasionally warmed by the periodic sun and quickly evaporating. Gray white clouds fill the sky from horizon to horizon, predicting a constant rainfall. Waves are large in width but not in height, rocking the ship with their passage. (Temp H 39/5 L 37/3, Wind — 5–10 mph.)
21–40	Heavy rain from ebony clouds pummel the ship and those unfortunate enough to be on deck. Waves like great grayish-green hammers smash against the ship every minute. The overhead clouds descend to a point where they encase the ship in a large subterranean chamber. Wind plunges against the vessel and its sail, trying to tip it from the mast and rigging. All loose items on deck vie for attention from the crashing waves or the blustery wind. (Temp H 45/7 L 36/3, Wind — 35–45 mph. Characters moving on deck must succeed on a saving throw each round or be knocked prone and pushed 10 feet in a random direction. All exposed areas of the ship are lightly obscured.)
41–60	The sky carries a darker shade than normal, clouds so thick they block out all trace of light. Rain is propelled horizontally with the wind, hitting like daggers and needles, reducing vision to mere feet around each person. Winds blow loose objects and people unprepared for its force off course. Waves 15–30 feet high assault the ship, blowing over the rail and soaking sailors with its frigid embrace. (Temp H 42/6 L 40/4, Wind — 45–50 mph. Characters moving on deck must succeed on a saving throw with a –1 penalty each round or be knocked prone and pushed 15 feet in a random direction. All exposed areas of the ship are lightly obscured.)
61–80	A constant rain falls from gray clouds overhead, keeping all within it thoroughly soaked. The wind propels the ship slowly, seemingly held back by the rain, over the large hillock-shaped waves. Occasional lightning flashes illuminate the depth of the rain, looking like iron bars for as far as the eye can see, peppering the water. (Temp H 42/6 L 35/2, Wind — 5–10 mph. Characters moving on deck must succeed on a saving throw each round or be knocked prone. All exposed areas of the ship are lightly obscured.)
81–00	The drone of the rain on the wooden deck becomes hypnotic after a time. The wind is not strong enough to alter the vertical direction of the rain, letting the sail hang like a soaked rag from the mast. The subtle waves rock the ship almost undetectably as they move by on unseen currents. Clouds looking like an inverted mountain range press down upon the ship and crew. (Temp H 48/10 L 40/4, Wind — 5–10 mph.)

Rain/Night

01–20	Lightning-rippled clouds streak by overhead; waves lift like cliffs (six to 15 feet) around the vessel. Large rain drops alternate from side-to-side and straight down with the force of a hammer blow. Rivers of water course around the deck from the rain and waves, creating treacherous footing for all on board. The sails snap and crack as it fills with the wind, dropping deluges of collected rain to the deck below. Periodically, the sky lights up with a lightning blast nearby, painting everything in shades of white and gray; all other times, the charcoal sky and water bestow a sense of isolation. (Temp H 36/3 L 26/ –3, Wind — 30–35 mph. Characters moving on deck must succeed on a saving throw with a –1 penalty each round or be knocked prone and pushed 15 feet in a random direction. All exposed areas of the ship are lightly obscured.)

21–40 A constant rain falls from gray clouds overhead, keeping all within thoroughly soaked. The wind propels the ship slowly, seemingly held in check by the rain, over the large hillock-shaped waves. Occasional lightning flashes illuminate the depth of the rain, looking like fine iron bars for as far as the eye can see, peppering the water. (Temp H 43/6 L 31/0, Wind — 5–10 mph. Characters moving on deck must succeed on a saving throw each round or be knocked prone. All exposed areas of the ship are lightly obscured.)

41–60 Thick, rolling clouds erupt continuously with thunder and rain, beating upon the wooden planks. The percussion of the rain is accented with the occasional spray of mountainous waves carried on the wind. Gusts of wind blow across the ship and attempt to pull everything along in its wake. Sight is reduced to feet, distance eliminated with thick sheets of rain. (Temp H 41/5 L 38/3, Wind — 30–50 mph. Characters moving on deck must succeed on a saving throw each round or be knocked prone and pushed 10 feet in a random direction. All exposed areas of the ship are heavily obscured.)

61–80 Hurricane force rain and winds pound the ship, which is tossed like a child's doll. Huge waves like mountains threaten to topple the vessel and launch the sailors into the unforgiving sea. Wind blows fiercely, lifting all heavy objects or small creatures not lashed down and propelling them around and off the ship. The sky and water are undistinguishable, erasing the horizon as both are steel gray. (Temp H 35/2 L 29/–2, Wind — 80–90 mph. Characters moving on deck must succeed on a saving throw with a –2 penalty each round or be knocked prone and pushed 20 feet in a random direction. All exposed areas of the ship are lightly obscured.)

81–00 A simple rain falls, creating a drumbeat of rain on the wooden deck. The wind is not strong enough to alter the vertical direction of the rain, letting the sail hang like a soaked rag from the mast. The subtle waves rock the ship almost undetectably as they move on under currents. Clouds looking like an inverted mountain range press down upon the ship and crew. Navigation can only be done through compass or landmarks. (Temp H 37/3 L 28/–2, Wind — 5–10 mph.)

Dry/Day

01–20 The large sun governs the sky, but a swift breeze keeps the temperature to a cooler level. Spray is pulled up from the many waves, capped in white froth and thrown across the deck. The horizon is marked with a large bank of gray clouds, promising rain in the next day or two. (Temp H 47/8 L 39/4, Wind — 20–25 mph.)

21–40 The sky is clear, dotted with numerous small, unimposing puffs of cloud. A steady wind blows, determined to cart items away in its embrace. The sun, high overhead, seems at a greater distance than usual given the lack of heat generated. Abundant waves run to the horizon, making up for size with numbers. The water is churned to a gray-green, and you can see only a few feet under the surface with any clarity, another indicator of the weak sun. (Temp H 43/6 L 33/1, Wind — 18–20 mph.)

41–60 A crystal-clear sky amplifies the sun, directing its heat against the ship and her crew. The wind puffs slowly, not enough to extinguish a candle let alone cool the flesh of those warmer than usual day. Waves move across the water like a herd, trying to carry the ship along in their wake, fighting the vessel should it try to turn away. The spray carries over the rail into the faces of those on deck, quickly drying to leave traces of powdered salt. (Temp H 40/4 L 35/2, Wind — 5–10 mph.)

61–80 Sun and gray clouds do battle overhead for dominance, sometimes plunging the ship into a dark twilight or bright daylight. Numerous waves about the size of a man run the length of the water as far as the eye can see, all topped with a cone of greenish-white froth. The wind picks this froth from each and carries it along, coating all surfaces. This cooling spray makes the trip enjoyable for most on board, even in the shade. The rigging and sails flap in the breeze, occasionally dropping additional sprays to the deck, glinting like jewels in the periodic sun. (Temp H 44/7 L 39/4, Wind — 18–20 mph.)

81–00 Gray the color of stone has been painted from horizon to horizon, plunging the day into twilight. The absence of wind allows the sails and rigging to hang lifeless, like cloth in a shop window. The water is unmarked, calm for many miles around the ship, with waves visible in the far distance. Pressure seems to build, raising the temperature over several hours to a more comfortable level. (Temp H 37/3 L 32/0, Wind — 5–10 mph. Reroll in four game hours on the wet–day chart for the approaching storm.)

Dry/Night

01–20 Clear sky provides a view of the numerous constellations and guiding stars. Wind gusts from the east, creating a flapping staccato to match the waves breaking on the hull of the ship. Whitecapped waves, visible in the moonlight, reach for the sailors on board, topping seven to eight feet. A slight mist can be felt in the wind; consequently, all surfaces are slick and shiny with moisture (Temp H 38/4 L 31/0, Wind — 15–25 mph. Characters moving on deck must succeed on a saving throw check each round or be knocked prone.)

21–40 Clear ebony night overhead provides astronomers and navigators a fine view of the stars and planets. A gentle wind blows from the south, flapping the sail and nettings. Small waves lap against the side of the boat like a heartbeat; small whitecaps stand out stark against the black background of the water and night sky. (Temp H 41/5 L 36/3, Wind — 15–25 mph.)

41–60 An overcast sky blocks the view of all but the brightest stars and planets. Some navigation can still be done by experienced sailors. A breeze comes and goes, proving to be a fickle asset for the sails on the ship, waves playing tag gently rock the ship back and forth. (Temp H 42/6 L 29/–2, Wind — 5–10 mph.)

61–80 Numerous stars turn the night sky into a twilight gray, offsetting the jet black of the calm water. A steady, soft wind blows, propelling the ship along on its way. The sound of the surf being cut by the hull is seemingly alone, periodically joined by the creak of the rigging and the soft voice of a sailor. (Temp H 45/7 L 39/4, Wind — 10–15 mph.)

81–00 Gale force winds blow, threatening to rip the sail from the mast, propelling the vessel over the waves like a toy. Thick ribbons of cloud race overhead like gray gashes in the constellations. Many large waves run the length of vision, occasionally growing to such a large size (45 feet) that they threaten to topple the ship like flotsam. (Temp H 37/3 L 26/–3, Wind — 65–70 mph. Characters moving on deck must succeed on a saving throw each round or be knocked prone and pushed five feet in a random direction.)

ARCTIC

Wind chill is a real concern when the temperature drops below 32° F. Exposure to the wind risks frostbite for flesh. The effective temperature, for purposes of calculating potential harm caused by extreme cold, can be found in the Wind Chill Table.

RAIN/DAY

01–20 White gray clouds span from horizon to horizon, and periodic deluges of snow drop upon the water and the ship. The deck is quickly covered in a blanket of white snow, making progress slow around the ship. Finding equipment is difficult for the inexperienced sailor, boxes and barrels becoming nondescript objects in the snow. The wind moves the snow in various directions as it descends, moving the sails to half full with their strongest force. (Temp H –11/–24 L –16/–27, Wind — 0–5 mph. All exposed areas of the ship count as difficult terrain. See rules above for the consequences of exposure to extreme temperatures.)

21–40 Frozen rain drops like sheets of needles upon sailors in the open. The wind drives the sleet almost horizontally across the waves. Large mountains of water move across the area, threatening to bash the vessel into submission. The steel-gray sky rolls like the underside of a surf, promising many hours of attack. The rigging creaks and sails moan ominously in the barrage of the storm. Movement along the deck is perilous at best; those in the upper reaches of the vessel cling for their lives. (Temp H –15/–27 L –25/–31, Wind — 20–25 mph. Characters moving on deck must succeed on a saving throw each round or be knocked prone and pushed 10 feet in a random direction. All exposed areas of the ship are lightly obscured. See rules above for the consequences of exposure to extreme temperatures.)

41–60 Freezing mist falls like a cloud landing on the water. Wind is present but too weak to fill sails. Ice floes move on the sunken currents, dancing around the ship at great distances. Waves are subdued, seemingly moving in numerous directions, with no discernible pattern. Ice forms on most surfaces with extended exposure, sails and rigging becoming rigid and hazardous with each passing hour. (Temp H –12/–29 L –17/–28, Wind — 0–5 mph. Characters moving on deck must succeed on a saving throw each round or be knocked prone. All exposed areas of the ship are lightly obscured. See rules above for the consequences of exposure to extreme temperatures.)

61–80 Clouds pregnant with lightning streak by overhead, waves lift like cliffs (six to 15 feet) around the vessel. Rain alternates from side-to-side and straight down with the force of a hammer blow. Ice coats all exposed surfaces in minutes, creating treacherous areas on the ship and rigging. The sails snap and crack as they fill with the wind, snow, and ice, dropping chunks of ice to the deck below. Periodically, the sky lights up with a lightning blast nearby, painting everything in shades of white and gray; all other times, the charcoal sky and water bestow a sense of isolation. (Temp H –19/–29 L –22/–30, Wind — 35–40 mph. Characters moving on deck must succeed on a saving throw each round or be knocked prone and pushed 10 feet in a random direction. All exposed areas of the ship are lightly obscured. See rules above for the consequences of exposure to extreme temperatures.)

81–00 The sky carries a darker shade than normal, clouds so thick they block out all trace of light. Rain is propelled horizontally with the wind, hitting like daggers and needles, reducing vision to mere feet around each person. Ice forms on all surfaces, making passage difficult on deck. Winds blow loose objects and people unprepared for its force off course. Waves 15–30 feet high assault the ship, blowing over the rail and soaking sailors with its frigid embrace. (Temp H –16/–27 L –27/–33, Wind — 27–35 mph. Characters moving on deck must succeed on a saving throw each round or be knocked prone and pushed five feet in a random direction. All exposed areas of the ship are lightly obscured.)

RAIN/NIGHT

01–20 Clouds infused with lightning fill the sky around the ship, while waves lift like cliffs (six to 15 feet) around the vessel. Rain alternates from side-to-side and straight down with the force of a hammer blow. Ice coats all exposed surfaces, quickly creating treacherous areas on the ship and rigging. The sails snap and crack as it fills with the wind, snow, and ice, dropping chunks of ice to the deck below. Periodically, the sky lights up with a lightning blast nearby, painting everything in shades of white, blue, and gray; all other times the charcoal sky and water bestow a sense of isolation. (Temp H –25/–30 L –30/–34, Wind — 50–55 mph. Characters moving on deck must succeed on a saving throw each round or be knocked prone and pushed 10 feet in a random direction. All exposed areas of the ship are lightly obscured.)

21–40 Freezing mist falls like a cloud landing on the water. Wind is present but too weak to fill sails. Ice floes move on the sunken currents, dancing around the ship at great distances. Waves are subdued, seemingly moving in numerous directions, no pattern discernible. Ice forms on most surfaces with extended exposure, sails and rigging becoming rigid and hazardous with each passing hour. (Temp H –12/–24 L –22/–30, Wind — 0–5 mph. Characters moving on deck must succeed on a saving throw each round or be knocked prone. All exposed areas of the ship are lightly obscured. See rules above for the consequences of exposure to extreme temperatures.)

41–60 The night sky carries a darker shade than normal, with clouds so thick they block out all trace of light. Rain is propelled horizontally with the wind, hitting like daggers and needles, reducing vision to mere feet around each person. Ice forms on all surfaces, making passage difficult on deck. Winds blow loose objects and people unprepared for its force off course. Waves 15–30 feet high assault the ship, blowing over the rail and soaking sailors with its frigid embrace. (Temp H –17/–28 L –24/–30, Wind — 27–35 mph. Characters moving on deck must succeed on a saving throw with a –1 penalty each round or be knocked prone and pushed 15 feet in a random direction. All exposed areas of the ship are heavily obscured.)

61–80 Constant icy drizzle settles on all surfaces, turning the dark night into a dark gray, reducing vision to nearly nonexistent. Frigid temperatures freeze the moisture within minutes on every surface. Travel across deck is difficult but manageable to those familiar with surroundings. Sound is subdued with the ice pellets, adding a muffling effect to conversations. Waves are unseen but can be felt hitting the ship every few seconds, occasionally bathing the deck with its spray, a testament to its height of several feet. (Temp H –16/–27 L –25/–31, Wind — 5–10 mph. Characters moving on deck must succeed on a saving throw each round or be knocked prone and pushed five feet in a random direction. All exposed areas of the ship are heavily obscured. See rules above for the consequences of exposure to extreme temperatures.)

81–00 Large thick flakes drop around the ship, landing softly on the water before melting. Equipment and decking are quickly covered in a thick blanket of white snow. Waves roll languidly, topping six feet in height but not steep enough to make more than an exaggerated rocking motion. A light wind blows carrying the flakes on the air currents, visible in the occasional moonlight. (Temp H –20/–29 L –26/–32, Wind — 5–10 mph. Characters moving on deck must succeed on a saving throw each round or be knocked prone. All exposed areas of the ship are lightly obscured.)

Dry/Day

01–20	Clear blue sky overhead provides ample room for the bright sun to shine. Wind gusts from the northeast, flapping the sail and nettings. Whitecapped waves topping seven to eight feet high seem to pus large chunks of ice along in their grasp. (Temp H –19/–29 L –24/–31, Wind — 20–25 mph. Those working while facing the sun must succeed on a saving throw or be blinded for 1d4 hours. Characters with a natural sensitivity to light take a –1 penalty on this saving throw. There is a 10% chance of a course change being required for an ice floe in the path of the ship.)
21–40	Sun and gray clouds do battle overhead for dominance, sometimes plunging the day into a gray twilight or bright daylight. Numerous waves about the size of a man run the length of the water as far as the eye can see, all topped with a cone of blue-white froth. The wind picks this froth from each and carries it along and freezes it to any surface it covers. The rigging and sails labor under the extra weight of the ice, glinting like jewels in the periodic sun. (Temp H –21/–29 L –28/–33, Wind — 20–25 mph. Characters moving on deck must succeed on a saving throw each round or be knocked prone. There is a 12% chance of a course change being required for an ice floe in the path of the ship.)
41–60	Gray the color of stone has been painted from horizon to horizon, plunging the day into twilight. The absence of wind allows the sails and rigging to hang listless, like cloth in a shop window. The water is unmarked, calm for many miles around the ship, with waves visible in the far distance. Pressure seems to build, raising the temperature over several hours to a more comfortable level. Icebergs in the distance hold steady like islands. (Temp H –18/–28 L –25/–31, Wind — 0–5 mph. Experienced sailors know a storm is coming. Reroll on Arctic day–rain chart in 1d4 hours for result. There is a 2% chance of a course change being required for icebergs in the path of the ship.)
61–80	Streamers of billowy clouds race overhead in the wind. Large waves buffet the ship and attempt to carry it along with them. Wind assaults the vessel hard from the west, never wavering or letting up. Tacking into the wind seems impossible from its vicious force while tracking with the wind runs a risk of never getting back control of the ship. (Temp H –18/–28 L –30/–34, Wind — 50–55 mph. Characters moving on deck must succeed on a saving throw each round or be knocked prone and pushed 10 feet in a random direction.)
81–00	The air burns with the wind chill, crusting ice all over the ship, with the sun adding no aid to the frigid temperature. Clouds are nonexistent in the sky, collecting only on the horizons. While filling the sails, the wind steals the breath from those on deck, freezing exposed flesh in minutes. (Temp H –16/–27 L –29/–34, Wind — 45–50 mph S. Characters moving on deck must succeed on a saving throw each round or be knocked prone and pushed 10 feet in a random direction.)

Dry/Night

01–20	Clear ebony night overhead provides astronomers and navigators a fine view of the stars and planets. A gentle wind blows from the south, flapping the sail and nettings. Small waves lap against the side of the boat like a heartbeat, and icebergs stand out stark white against the black background of the water and night sky. (Temp H –20/–29 L –27/–33, Wind — 5–10 mph. There is a 10% chance of a course change being required for an ice floe in the path of the ship.)
21–40	Large clouds move overhead, blocking the stars and moon with their bulk. The ship rolls gently on the waves as it rides through the water. Occasionally larger waves provide a small drop for the vessel as it is carried over the lip of the wave. The strong wind takes the ship along with it, filling the fails and pulling at cloaks of those on board. (Temp H –17/–28 L –25/–31, Wind — 40–45 mph.)
41–60	Clouds block all stars and only hint at the location of the moon, adding a claustrophobic feel to the trip. The absence of wind allows the sails and rigging to hang listless like cloth in a shop window. The ebony water ripples in the soft breeze, whitecaps standing out like glowing embers. (Temp H –14/–26 L –28/–33, Wind — 0–5 mph. There is a 2% chance of a course change being required for icebergs in the path of the ship.)
61–80	Partial clouds cover sections of the sky, seemingly unmoving. Large waves buffet the ship and attempt to bear it along with them. Wind assaults the vessel hard from the west, never wavering or letting up. Travel during the night at full sail runs a double risk of colliding with ice. (Temp H –19/–29 L –25/–31, Wind — 45–50 mph. Characters moving on deck must succeed on a saving throw each round or be knocked prone and pushed 10 feet in a random direction. There is a 15% chance of a course change being required for ice.)
81–00	Wisps of cloud move across the sky, sometimes blocking the stars. The brightness of the visible stars and moon provides ample light to maneuver around the ship and perform most tasks. The ever-present wind provides enough force to keep the ship moving at optimum speed. The absence of spray from the calm waters allows for equipment to remain cold but dry. (Temp H –25/–31 L –35/–37, Wind — 10–15 mph.)

EQUATORIAL

Within the Equatorial region, humidity is an issue for temperature measurement. Reference the Humidity Table to bring about a more realistic gauge for temperature; consequently, the effects of heat upon those traveling the waves should be watched closely.

Rain/Day

01–20	A heavy wind blows, adding a texture to the warm rain falling. Large drops patter along the deck, and occasional sunshine warms the deck, quickly evaporating the rain and adding to the humidity. A sticky aspect of the air grows throughout the day as the humidity rises. Sunlight glints off the water like numerous smaller suns, blinding those not ready for the effect. Waves are large in width but not in height, rocking the ship with their passage. (Temp H 75/24 L 58/15, Wind — 20–25 mph.)
21–40	Driving rain pummels the ship and those on board, quickly soaking all equipment and people. The waves are sedated, rarely topping five feet, seemingly held down with the impact of the rain. The sun tries to pierce the cloud cover with its intense glare, only succeeding in raising the temperature. Wind is nonexistent, hammered to submission by the heavy rain. (Temp H 77/25 L 63/17, Wind — 0–5 mph.)
41–60	Seemingly in rhythm with the lapping waves, periodic rain drops in vast amounts, quickly soaking all surfaces and washing away loose items. Between rainfalls, the sun attempts to burn away the moisture with blistering heat, never quite successful and so leaving all with a heaviness of moisture. Waves roll languidly, topping six feet in height but not steep enough to make more than an exaggerated rocking motion. The wind blows merrily, billowing out the sails of the ship and propelling the vessel over the large waves. (Temp H 79/27 L 71/22, Wind — 10–15 mph. Characters moving on deck during a deluge must succeed on a saving throw or be knocked prone and pushed 10 feet in a random direction.)
61–80	A drizzle of rain, sometimes hard and sometimes light, falls throughout the day. All surfaces are thoroughly soaked and heavy with water. The warmth of the occasional sun is diminished slightly by the cool rain, keeping it tolerable for all involved. Waves are present but pose no threat to the navigation of the ship or to the course she desires to take. The wind blows constantly, keeping the sails full but not pushing the limit of its capabilities. (Temp H 76/25 L 66/19, Wind — 30–35 mph.)

81–00	Rain drops like a swarm of arrows carried at a velocity that actually inflicts pain on exposed skin. Waves like great gray-green boulders smash against the ship every minute. The overhead clouds descend to a point where it seems the ship is in a large chamber. Wind hurtles against the vessel and its sail, trying to rip it free from the mast and rigging. All loose items are tossed around the decking, creating hazards for those on deck. (Temp H 73/22 L 62/17, Wind — 60–65 mph. Characters moving on deck must succeed on a saving throw each round or be knocked prone and pushed 10 feet in a random direction.)

Rain/Night

01–20	The humidity of the night is made comfortable by the patter of rain upon the deck. The coolness of the rain seems to steal some of the thickness in the air. The thin clouds mask the presence of the stars but leave a large halo where the moon tries to shine. The waves crash against the hull as if trying to keep the ship from reaching its goal. The bounce of the ship as it passes over the waves keeps all but the soundest sleepers awake. (Temp H 73/22 L 57/14, Wind — 0–5 mph.)
21–40	Heavy rain from ebony clouds press down on the ship and those on deck. Waves can be seen in the dark like great gray-green boulders that smash against the ship every minute. The overhead clouds descend to a point where it seems the ship is in a large gray bubble. Wind hurtles against the vessel and its sail, trying to rip it from the mast and rigging. All loose items on deck vie for attention from the crashing waves or the blustery wind. (Temp H 71/21 L 68/20, Wind — 50–60 mph. Characters moving on deck must succeed on a saving throw each round or be knocked prone and pushed 10 feet in a random direction. All exposed areas of the ship are lightly obscured.)
41–60	Seemingly in rhythm with the lapping waves, periodic rain drops in vast amounts, quickly soaking all surfaces and washing away loose materials. Waves roll languidly, topping six feet in height but not steep enough to make more than an exaggerated rocking motion. A light wind blows, carrying a humid mist from the still warm water, visible in the intermittent moonlight. (Temp H 72/22 L 65/15, Wind — 5–10 mph. Characters moving on deck must succeed on a saving throw each round or be knocked prone. All exposed areas of the ship are lightly obscured.)
61–80	A drizzle of rain, sometimes hard and sometimes light, falls continuously throughout during the nighttime hours. All surfaces are thoroughly soaked and heavy with water. The warmth of the day rapidly disappears and is replaced with the humidity of the still evaporating water around the ship. The waves are smaller than normal and work with the rain to stay weak enough to be inconsequential. The wind blows constantly, keeping the sails full but not pushing the limit of its capabilities. (Temp H 71/21 L 66/19, Wind — 20–25 mph.)
81–00	A thrashing rain accompanies hurricane force winds. In the distance amid lightning flashes, waterspouts can be seen reaching for the sky. Waves the size of small mountains rise above the vessel, giving the ship a wide span of view when atop a wave and a sense of claustrophobia when in a gully. (Temp H 74/24 L 64/18, Wind — 70–75 mph. Characters moving on deck must succeed on a saving throw with a –1 penalty each round or be knocked prone and pushed 15 feet in a random direction. All exposed areas of the ship are lightly obscured.)

Dry/Day

01–20	The large sun dominates the sky, but a swift breeze keeps the temperature to a more moderate level. Spray is pulled up from the many waves, capped in white froth. The horizon is marked with a large range of gray clouds that promise rain in the next day or two. The humidity rises throughout the day, adding a weight to the sun that saps the strength of those not acquainted with the equatorial waters. (Temp H 76/25 L 64/18, Wind — 30–35 mph.)

21–40	Clouds run amok along the sky, occasionally blocking the sun and its warmth. The wind seemingly growls as it tears across the water at the ship. The sail quivers, trying to keep the wind from escaping. Waves rise up and crash against the hull of the ship, each impact like a bludgeon from nature itself. (Temp H 77/26 L 74/24, Wind — 25–35 mph. Characters moving on a deck must succeed on a saving throw each round or be knocked prone. All exposed areas of the ship are lightly obscured.)
41–60	A crystal-clear sky seems to enlarge the sun, which directs its heat against the ship and her crew. The wind puffs slowly, not enough to extinguish a candle, let alone cool the flesh of those in the open. Waves move across the water like a herd, trying to carry the ship along in their wake, fighting the vessel should it try to turn away. The spray carries over the rail into the faces of those on deck, quickly drying to leave powdered salt. (Temp H 77/26 L 70/21, Wind — 0–5 mph.)
61–80	The thick clouds overhead threaten to release their burden, moisture released in the form of a thick, palpable air. While no rain has fallen during the day, all surfaces are beaded with sweat and spray from the moisture-laced air. The moderate wind moves both the ship and the clouds, lifting the waves to heights of 10 feet, launching the spray into the air. The ship rolls with the impact as it tips down one wave and up another, the prow having difficulty cutting through the water. (Temp H 71/21 L 58/15, Wind — 10–15 mph.)
81–00	The sky is clear and dotted with numerous small, unimposing puffs of cloud. A steady wind blows, determined to cart items away in its embrace. The sun, high overhead, seems at a greater distance than usual given the lack of heat generated. Abundant waves run to the horizon, making up for size with numbers. The water is churned to a gray-green, and you can see only a few feet under the surface with any clarity, another indicator of the weak sun. (Temp H 73/22 L 67/19, Wind — 25–30 mph.)

Dry/Night

01–20	Clear expanse provides a view of the numerous constellations and guiding stars. Wind gusts from the south, creating a flapping staccato to match the waves breaking on the hull of the ship. Whitecapped waves, visible in the moonlight, reach for the sailors on board, topping seven to eight feet. A slight mist can be felt in the wind; consequently, all surfaces are slick and shiny with moisture. (Temp H 75/25 L 64/18, Wind — 15–25 mph. Characters moving on deck must succeed on a saving throw each round or be knocked prone.)
21–40	Clouds of stone gray run from horizon to horizon, extinguishing the stars and moon from view. The absence of wind allows the sails and rigging to hang listless, like cloth in a shop window. The water is unmarked, calm for many miles around the ship, with waves visible in the far distance. Pressure seems to build, raising the temperature over several hours to just above a comfortable level. (Temp H 77/25 L 58/15, Wind — 0–5 mph. Experienced sailors know a storm is coming. Reroll on Equatorial day–rain chart in 1d4 hours for result.)
41–60	The cool of the night is identified by the daytime heat escaping the decking, misting the moisture collected through the daylight hours. Besides raising the humidity to an uncomfortable level, it also deadens the night sounds of the creaking riggings and lapping waves. Long trenches of waves roll the ship as it moves through them like long strides of a great beast. Occasional clouds plunge the ship into darkness, allowing the moon and stars to peer through again in a few moments. (Temp H 73/22 L 65/18, Wind — 10–20 mph.)

| 61–80 | Stars and gray clouds do battle overhead for control, sometimes plunging the world into a dark twilight or bright moonlight. Numerous waves about the size of a man run the length of the water as far as the eye can see, all topped with a small cone of greenish-white froth. The rigging and sails have rivulets of collected water, which pools on the deck. Lines are heavy with water, and deck boards are slick and shiny, sometimes reflecting the occasional moonlight. (Temp H 74/24 L 56/14, Wind — 20–25 mph. Characters moving on deck must succeed on a saving throw each round or be knocked prone.) |
| 81–00 | Clear ebony night overhead provides astronomers and navigators a fine view of the stars and planets. A gentle wind blows from the south-southeast, flapping the sail and nettings. Small waves lap against the side of the boat like a heartbeat, reflections of the moon on the waves stand out stark white against the black background of the water and night sky. (Temp H 78/25 L 67/19, Wind — 5–10 mph.) |

AUTUMN

TROPICAL

Heatstroke is a risk for any who travel the warm regions of the world. Those exerting themselves must succeed on a saving throw for each hour of strenuous work or become exhausted (–1 to hit, damage and saves). For each cumulative hour of strenuous work, the save is made with a cumulative –1 penalty. Resting in shaded areas for 10 minutes per hour negates the –1 penalty for that hour. Spell components run a 10% chance of spoiling in humidity, if you determine they are subject to such damage.

RAIN/DAY

01–20	A gentle breeze blows, adding a pleasant cooling to the warm rain falling. Large drops patter along the deck and occasional sunshine warms the deck, quickly evaporating the rain and adding to the humidity. A sticky aspect of the air grows throughout the day as the humidity rises. Sunlight glints off the water like numerous smaller suns, blinding those not ready for the effect. Waves are large in width but not in height, rocking the ship with their passage. (Temp H 90/33 L 78/26, Wind — 10–15 mph.)
21–40	Severe rain pummels the ships and those on board, quickly soaking all equipment and people. The waves are sedate, rarely topping five feet and seemingly held down by the rain. The sun tries to pierce the cloud cover with its intense glare, but only succeeds in raising the temperature. Wind is nonexistent, hammered to submission by the heavy rain. (Temp H 89/32 L 84/30, Wind — 0–5 mph.)
41–60	Seemingly in rhythm with the lapping waves, periodic rain drops in large amounts, quickly soaking all surfaces and washing away loose items. Between rainfalls, the sun attempts to burn away the moisture with searing heat. Waves roll languidly, topping six feet in height but not steep enough to make more than an exaggerated rocking motion. The wind blows merrily, billowing out the sails of the ship and propelling the vessel over the large waves. (Temp H 88/32 L 74/24, Wind — 20–25 mph. Characters moving on deck during a deluge must succeed on a saving throw each round or be knocked prone and pushed 10 feet in a random direction.)
61–80	A drizzle of rain, sometimes hard and sometimes light, falls continuously throughout the day. All surfaces are thoroughly soaked and heavy with water. The warmth of the occasional sun is diminished slightly by the cool rain, keeping it tolerable for all involved. The wind blows constantly, keeping the sails full but not pushing the limit of its capabilities. (Temp H 86/31 L 79/27, Wind — 30–35 mph.)

| 81–00 | Rain from imposing clouds strike the ship and those on deck. Waves like great gray-green boulders smash against the ship every minute or so. The overhead clouds descend to a point where it seems the ship is in a large chamber. Wind hurtles against the vessel and its sail, trying to rip it from the mast and rigging. All loose items on deck vie for attention from the crashing waves or the blustery wind. (Temp H 85/30 L 75/25, Wind — 45–50 mph. Characters moving on deck must succeed on a saving throw each round or be knocked prone and pushed 10 feet in a random direction. All exposed areas of the ship are lightly obscured.) |

RAIN/NIGHT

01–20	The cool of the night is accompanied by the patter of rain upon the deck. The humidity keeps the coolness of the night from becoming entirely comfortable. The moon makes itself known through the clouds, illuminating a portion of the night sky to milky white. The waves crash against the hull as if trying to keep the ship from reaching its goal. The bounce of the ship as it passes over the waves keeps all but the soundest sleepers awake. (Temp H 84/30 L 74/24, Wind — 15–20 mph.)
21–40	Steady rainfall beats at the ship with determination normally reserved for the cursed. Waves can be seen in the dark like a herd of turquoise animals, smashing against the ship every minute. Wind plunges against the vessel and its sails, trying to rip it from its bindings. All loose items and small creatures on deck vie for attention from the crashing waves or the blustery wind. (Temp H 87/31 L 81/28, Wind — 60–65 mph. Characters moving on deck must succeed on a saving throw each round or be knocked prone and pushed 10 feet in a random direction. All exposed areas of the ship are lightly obscured.)
41–60	Sheets of rain drop upon the water and the unfortunate seagoing vessel, completely waterlogging the ship and her crew. Occasionally easing off in intensity, the rain soon begins again, ramping up its strength. Waves roll languidly, topping six feet in height but not steep enough to make a difference in any ship's course should it attempt to climb its expanse. A light wind blows, carrying mist from the still warm water, visible in the occasional moonlight. (Temp H 83/29 L 79/27, Wind — 5–10 mph. Characters moving on deck during a deluge must succeed on a saving throw each round or be knocked prone and pushed 10 feet in a random direction. All exposed areas of the ship are lightly obscured.)
61–80	A light drizzle of rain falls from gray clouds overhead, keeping all within it thoroughly soaked. The wind propels the ship slowly, seemingly held back by the rain, over the large hillock-shaped waves. Occasional lightning flashes illuminate the depth of the rain, looking like iron bars for as far as the eye can see, peppering the water. (Temp H 77/26 L 68/21, Wind — 15–20 mph.)
81–00	A continual rain falls from gray clouds overhead, keeping all within it thoroughly soaked. The wind propels the ship slowly, seemingly held back by the rain, over the large hillock-shaped waves. Occasional lightning flashes illuminate the depth of the rain, looking like iron bars for as far as the eye can see, peppering the water. (Temp H 77/26 L 68/21, Wind — 15–20 mph. Characters moving on deck must succeed on a saving throw each round or be knocked prone. All exposed areas of the ship are lightly obscured.)

DRY/DAY

| 01–20 | The large sun dominates the sky, but a swift breeze keeps the temperature to a more moderate level. Spray is pulled up from the many waves, capped in white froth and tossed upon the ship and anything on deck. The horizon is marked with a large bank of gray clouds that promise rain in the next day or two. (Temp H 88/32 L 75/24, Wind — 20–25 mph.) |

21–40	Clouds run amok along the sky, occasionally blocking the sun and its warmth. The wind seemingly growls as it tears across the water at the ship. The sail quivers, trying to keep the wind from escaping. Waves rise up and crash against the hull of the ship, each impact like a bludgeon from nature itself. (Temp H 86/31 L 79/27, Wind — 25–35 mph.)
41–60	A crystal clear sky magnifies the sun, directing its heat against the ship and her crew. The wind puffs slowly, not enough to extinguish a candle, let alone cool the flesh of those in the open. Waves move across the water like a herd, trying to carry the ship along in their wake, fighting the vessel should it try to turn away. The spray carries over the rail into the faces of those on deck, quickly drying to leave powdered salt. (Temp H 90/33 L 84/30, Wind — 0–5 mph.)
61–80	The thick clouds overhead threaten to release their burden but maintain their hold for now. The moderate wind moves both the ship and the clouds, lifting waves to heights of 10 feet and launching the spray into the air. The ship rolls with the impacts as it tips down one wave and up another, the prow having difficulty cutting through the water. (Temp H 84/30 L 79/27, Wind — 15–20 mph.)
81–00	The sky is clear, dotted with numerous small, unimposing puffs of cloud. A steady wind blows, determined to cart items away in its embrace. The sun, high overhead, seems at a greater distance than usual given the lack of heat generated. Abundant waves run to the horizon, making up for size with numbers. The water is churned to a gray-green, and you can see only a few feet under the surface with any clarity, another indicator of the weak sun. (Temp H 79/27 L 77/26, Wind — 30–35 mph.)

Dry/Night

01–20	Clear sky provides a view of the numerous constellations and guiding stars. Wind gusts from the northeast, creating a flapping staccato to match the waves breaking on the hull of the ship. Whitecapped waves, visible in the moonlight, reach for the sailors on board, topping seven to eight feet. A slight mist can be felt in the wind; consequently, all surfaces are slick and shiny with moisture. (Temp H 80/27 L 79/27, Wind — 15–25 mph.)
21–40	Clouds of stone gray run from horizon to horizon, extinguishing the stars and moon from view. The absence of wind allows the sails and rigging to hang listless, like cloth in a shop window. The water is unmarked, calm for many miles around the ship, waves visible in the far distance. Pressure seems to build, raising the temperature over several hours to just above a comfortable level. (Temp H 81/28 L 77/26, Wind — 0–5 mph. Experienced sailors know a storm is coming. Reroll on Tropical day–rain chart in 1d4 hours for result.)
41–60	The cool of the night is easily identified by the daytime heat escaping the decking, misting the moisture collected through the daylight hours. Besides raising the humidity to an uncomfortable level, it also deadens the night sounds of the creaking riggings and lapping waves. Long trenches of water roll the ship as it moves through them like long strides of a great beast. Occasional clouds plunge the ship into darkness, allowing the moon and stars to peer through again in a few moments. (Temp H 85/30 L 83/29, Wind — 10–20 mph.)
61–80	Alternating cloud cover keeps the world in either the pitch dark or the luminescent twilight. Numerous waves, about the size of a large horse (eight feet), run the length of the water and as far as the eye can see, all topped with a cone of greenish-white froth. The rigging and sails have rivulets of collected water, which pools on the deck. Lines are heavy with water, and deck boards are slick and shiny, sometimes reflecting the occasional moonlight. (Temp H 78/26 L 75/24, Wind — 20–25 mph.)
81–00	Clear ebony night overhead provides astronomers and navigators a fine view of the stars and planets. A gentle wind blows from the west, flapping the sail and nettings. Small waves lap against the side of the boat like a heartbeat, reflections of the moon on the waves stand out stark white against the black background of the water and night sky. (Temp H 82/29 L 80/28, Wind — 5–10 mph.)

Temperate

01–20	A placid breeze blows, adding a slight chill to the damp air. Large drops patter along the deck, occasionally warmed by the periodic sun and quickly evaporating. Gray-white clouds fill the sky from horizon to horizon, predicting a constant rainfall. Waves are large in width but not in height, rocking the ship with their passage. (Temp H 75/25 L 63/18, Wind — 5–10 mph.)
21–40	Heavy rain from ebony clouds attack the ship and those unfortunate enough to be on deck. Waves like great gray-green hammers smash against the ship every minute. The overhead clouds descend to a point where they encase the ship in a world of twilight. Wind hurtles against the vessel and its sail, trying to rip it from the mast and rigging. All loose items on deck vie for attention from the crashing waves or the blustery wind. (Temp H 82/29 L 69/21, Wind — 50–60 mph. Characters moving on deck must succeed on a saving throw each round or be knocked prone and pushed 10 feet in a random direction.)
41–60	The sky carries a darker shade than normal, with clouds so thick they block out all trace of light. Rain is propelled horizontally with the wind, hitting like daggers and needles, reducing vision to mere feet around each person. Winds blow loose objects and people unprepared for its force off course. Waves 15–30 feet high assault the ship, blowing over the rail and soaking sailors with its frigid embrace. (Temp H 79/27 L 75/24, Wind — 45–50 mph NE. Characters moving on deck must succeed on a saving throw each round or be knocked prone and pushed five feet in a random direction. All exposed areas of the ship are lightly obscured.)
61–80	A constant rain falls from gray clouds overhead, keeping all within it thoroughly soaked. The wind propels the ship slowly, seemingly afraid to let its fury loose. Waves remain small and inconsequential, providing no hindrance to navigation or speed. Occasional lightning flashes illuminate the depth of the rain, looking like iron bars for as far as the eye can see, peppering the water. (Temp H 76/25 L 65/19, Wind — 5–10 mph. All exposed areas of the ship are lightly obscured.)
81–00	A simple rain falls, creating a constant drone of rain on the wooden deck. The wind is not strong enough to alter the vertical direction of the rain, letting the sail hang like a soaked rag from the mist. The subtle waves rock the ship almost undetectably as they move by on unseen currents. Clouds looking like an inverted mountain range press down upon the ship and crew. (Temp H 82/29 L 63/18, Wind — 5–10 mph.)

Rain/Night

01–20	Lightning-rippled clouds streak by overhead as waves lift like cliffs (six to 15 feet) around the vessel. Rain alternates from side-to-side and straight down with the force of a hammer blow. Rivers of water course around the deck from the rain and waves, creating treacherous footing for all on board. The sails snap and crack as they fill with wind, dropping deluges of collected rain to the deck below. Periodically, the sky lights up with a lightning blast nearby, painting everything in shades of white, blue, and gray; all other times, the charcoal sky and water bestow a sense of isolation. (Temp H 75/25 L 74/24, Wind — 20–25 mph. Characters moving on deck must succeed on a saving throw each round or be knocked prone and pushed five feet in a random direction. All exposed areas of the ship are lightly obscured.)

21–40	Rain constantly falls from gray clouds overhead, keeping all within it thoroughly soaked. The wind propels the ship slowly, seemingly held back by the rain, over the large hillock-shaped waves. Occasional lightning flashes illuminate the depth of the rain, looking like iron bars for as far as the eye can see, peppering the water. (Temp H 78/26 L 69/21, Wind — 5–10 mph. All exposed areas of the ship are lightly obscured.)
41–60	Thick, rolling clouds erupt constantly with thunder and rain, beating upon the wooden planks. The percussion of the rain is accented with the occasional spray of enormous waves carried on the wind. Gusts of wind blow across the ship, attempting to pull everything along in their wake. Sight is reduced to feet, while seeing into the distance is eliminated with the thick sheets of rain. (Temp H 76/25 L 63/18, Wind — 35–45 mph. Characters moving on deck must succeed on a saving throw each round or be knocked prone and pushed five feet in a random direction. All exposed areas of the ship are heavily obscured.)
61–80	Hurricane force rain and winds toss the ship like a doll during a child's tantrum. Huge waves like mountains threaten to topple the vessel and launch the sailors into the unforgiving sea. Wind blows fiercely, lifting all heavy objects or small creatures not lashed down and propelling them around and off the ship. The sky and water are indistinguishable, erasing the horizon and any gauge for distance. (Temp H 69/21 L 61/17, Wind — 55–60 mph. Characters moving on deck must succeed on a saving throw each round or be knocked prone and pushed 10 feet in a random direction.)
81–00	A simple rain falls, creating a constant drumming of rain on the wooden deck. The wind is not strong enough to alter the vertical direction of the rain, letting the sail hang like a soaked rag from the mast. The waves rock the ship almost lovingly as they move past, propelled by unseen currents. Clouds looking like an inverted mountain range press down upon the ship and crew. Navigation can be done only through compass or landmarks. (Temp H 74/124 L 68/21, Wind — 5–10 mph E.)

Dry/Day

01–20	The enormous sun dominates the sky, but a swift breeze keeps the temperature to a cooler level. Spray pulled up from the many waves capped in white froth is thrown across the deck. The horizon is marked with a large bank of gray clouds promising rain in the next day or two. (Temp H 78/26 L 70/22, Wind — 30–35 mph.)
21–40	The sky is clear and dotted with numerous small unimposing puffs of cloud. A solid wind blows, determined to cart items away in its embrace. The sun, high overhead, seems at a greater distance than usual given the lack of heat generated. Abundant waves run to the horizon, making up for size with numbers. The water is churned to a gray-green, and you can see only a few feet under the surface with any clarity, another indicator of the weak sun. (Temp H 76/25 L 69/21, Wind — 25–30 mph.)
41–60	A crystal-clear sky magnifies the sun, directing its heat against the ship and her crew. The wind puffs slowly, not enough to extinguish a candle let alone cool the flesh of those caught in the sun's angry flare. Waves move across the water like a herd, trying to carry the ship along in their wake, fighting the vessel should it try to turn away. The spray carries over the rail into the faces of those on deck, quickly drying to leave traces of powdered salt. (Temp H 82/29 L 74/24, Wind — 5–10 mph. Sunstroke occurs in 3d8 rounds unless properly attired for the sun.)

61–80	Sun and gray clouds do battle overhead for supremacy, sometimes plunging the water into a dark twilight or bright daylight. Numerous waves about the size of a man run the length of the water as far as the eye can see, all topped with a cone of white froth. The wind picks this froth from each and carries it along, coating all surfaces. This cooling spray makes the trip enjoyable for most on board, even in the shade. The rigging and sails labor, flapping in the breeze, occasionally dropping additional sprays to the deck, glinting like jewels in the periodic sun. (Temp H 75/25 L 67/20, Wind — 18–20 mph N.)
81–00	The sky resembles a great slab of granite from horizon to horizon, plunging the day into twilight. The absence of wind allows the sails and rigging to hang listless, like robes on a wizard. The water is unmarked, calm for many miles around the ship, with waves visible in the far distance. Pressure seems to build, raising the temperature over several hours to a more comfortable level. (Temp H 71/22 L 66/19, Wind — 5–10 mph. Reroll in four game hours on the wet-day chart for the approaching storm.)

Dry/Night

01–20	Clear sky provides a view of the numerous constellations and guiding stars. Wind gusts from the west to create a flapping staccato to match the waves breaking on the hull of the ship. Whitecapped waves, visible in the moonlight, reach for the sailors on board, topping seven to eight feet. A slight mist can be felt in the wind; consequently, all surfaces are slick and shiny with moisture. (Temp H 78/26 L 63/18, Wind — 15–25 mph.)
21–40	Clear ebony night overhead provides astronomers and navigators a fine view of the stars and planets. A gentle wind blows from the south, flapping the sail and nettings. Small waves lap against the side of the boat like a heartbeat; small whitecaps stand out stark against the black background of the water and night sky. (Temp H 80/28 L 66/19, Wind — 15–25 mph.)
41–60	An overcast sky blocks the view of all but the brightest stars and planets. Some navigation can still be done by experienced sailors. A breeze comes and goes, proving to be a fickle asset for the sails on the ship, and waves playing tag gently rock the ship back and forth. (Temp H 79/27 L 75/24, Wind — 5–10 mph.)
61–80	Numerous stars turn the onyx sky into a twilight gray, offsetting the jet black of the calm water. A steady, soft wind blows, propelling the ship along on its way. The sound of the surf being cut by the hull is seemingly alone, periodically joined by the creak of the rigging and the soft voice of a sailor. (Temp H 70/22 L 66/19, Wind — 10–15 mph.)
81–00	A severe wind blows, threatening to rip the sail from the mast, propelling the vessel over the waves like a plaything. Thick ribbons of clouds race overhead like gray gashes in the constellations. Many large waves run the length of the vision, occasionally growing to such a large size (45 feet) that they threaten to topple the ship like flotsam. (Temp H 69/21 L 61/17, Wind — 15–25 mph.)

ARCTIC

Wind chill is a real concern when the temperature drops below 32° F. Exposure to the wind risks frostbite for flesh. The effective temperature, for purposes of calculating potential harm caused by extreme cold, can be found in the Wind Chill Table.

RAIN/DAY

01–20	White-gray clouds span from horizon to horizon, and periodic deluges of snow drop upon the water and the ship. The deck is quickly covered in a blanket of white snow, making progress slow around the ship. Finding equipment is difficult for the inexperienced sailor, with boxes and barrels becoming nondescript objects in the snow. The wind moves the snow in various directions as it descends, moving the sails to half full with their strongest force. (Temp H 29/–2 L 21/–6, Wind — 10–15 mph.)
21–40	Sleet drops like sheets of needles upon sailors in the open. The wind drives the sleet almost horizontally across the waves. Large mountains of water move across the area, threatening to bash the vessel into submission. The steel gray sky rolls like the underside of a surf, promising many hours of attack. The rigging creaks and sails moan ominously in the barrage of the storm. Movement along the deck is perilous at best; those in the upper reaches of the vessel cling for their lives. (Temp H 23/–5 L 20/–4, Wind — 35–40 mph. Characters moving on deck must succeed on a saving throw each round or be knocked prone and pushed 10 feet in a random direction. All exposed areas of the ship are lightly obscured.)
41–60	Freezing mist falls like a cloud landing on the water. Wind is present but is too weak to fill sails. Ice floes move on the sunken currents, dancing around the ship at great distances. Waves are subdued, seemingly moving in numerous directions with no pattern discernible. Ice forms on most surfaces with extended exposure, with sails and rigging becoming rigid and hazardous with each passing hour. (Temp H 28/–3 L 21/–6 Wind — 0–5 mph. Characters moving on deck must succeed on a saving throw each round or be knocked prone. All exposed areas of the ship are lightly obscured.)
61–80	Crimson lightning tears through the clouds, streaking by overhead, and waves lift like cliffs (six to 15 feet) around the vessel. Rain alternates from side-to-side and straight down with the force of a hammer blow. Ice coats all exposed surfaces in minutes, creating treacherous areas on the ship and rigging. The sails snap and crack as they fill with the wind, snow, and ice, dropping chunks of ice to the deck below. Periodically, the sky lights up with a lightning blast nearby painting everything in shades of white and black; all other times the charcoal sky and water bestow a sense of isolation. (Temp H 31/0 L 23/–4, Wind — 50–55 mph. Characters moving on deck must succeed on a saving throw each round or be knocked prone and pushed 10 feet in a random direction. All exposed areas of the ship are lightly obscured.)
81–00	The sky carries a darker shade than normal, with clouds so thick they block out all trace of light. Hail is propelled horizontally with the wind, hitting like daggers and needles, reducing vision to mere feet around each person. Ice forms on all surfaces, making passage difficult on deck. Winds blow loose objects and people unprepared for its force off course. Waves 15–30 feet high assault the ship, blowing over the rail and soaking sailors with its frigid embrace. (Temp H 33/1 L 27/–2, Wind — 35–40 mph. Characters moving on deck must succeed on a saving throw each round or be knocked prone and pushed 10 feet in a random direction.)

RAIN/NIGHT

01–20	Lightning-rippled clouds streak by overhead. Waves lift like cliffs (six to 15 feet) around the vessel as rain attacks side-to-side and straight down with the force of a hammer blow. Ice coats all exposed surfaces quickly, creating treacherous areas on the ship and rigging. The sails resound with snaps and cracks as they fill with the wind, snow, and ice, dropping chunks of ice to the deck below. Periodically the sky lights up with a violet or crimson lightning blast nearby, painting everything with shades of white; all other times, the charcoal sky and water bestow a sense of isolation. (Temp H 28/–2 L 21/–6, Wind — 25–35 mph. Characters moving on deck must succeed on a saving throw each round or be knocked prone and pushed five feet in a random direction. There is a 10% chance of a course change being required for ice formation in the path of the ship.)
21–40	Icy mist falls like a cloud, landing on the water. Wind is present but too weak to fill sails. Ice floes move on the sunken currents, dancing around the ship like predators at great distances. Waves are subdued, seemingly moving in numerous directions, with no discernible pattern. Ice forms on most surfaces with extended exposure, and sails and rigging become rigid and hazardous with each passing hour. (Temp H 30/–1 L 23/–5, Wind — 0–5 mph. Characters moving on deck must succeed on a saving throw each round or be knocked prone. All exposed areas of the ship are lightly obscured.)
41–60	The night sky carries a shade darker than normal, with clouds so thick they block out all trace of light. Rain is propelled horizontally with the wind, hitting like daggers and needles, reducing vision to mere feet around each person. Ice forms on all surfaces, making passage dangerous on deck and in the lines above. Winds blow loose objects and people unprepared for its force off course. Waves 15–30 feet high assault the ship, blowing over the rail and soaking sailors with its frigid embrace. (Temp H 33/1 L 23/–5, Wind — 27–35 mph. Characters moving on deck must succeed on a saving throw each round or be knocked prone and pushed 10 feet in a random direction. All exposed areas of the ship are heavily obscured.)
61–80	Constant sub-zero drizzle settles on all surfaces, turning the dark night into a dark gray, reducing vision to nearly nonexistent. Frigid temperatures freeze the moisture within minutes on every surface. Travel across the deck is difficult but manageable to those familiar with the surroundings. Sound is subdued with the ice pellets, adding a muffling effect to conversations. Waves are unseen but can be felt hitting the ship every few seconds, occasionally bathing the deck with its spray, a testament to its height of several feet. (Temp H 28/–2 L 21/–6, Wind — 5–10 mph. Characters moving on deck must succeed on a saving throw each round or be knocked prone and pushed 10 feet in a random direction. All exposed areas of the ship are heavily obscured.)
81–00	Large thick flakes drop around the ship, landing softly on the water before melting. Equipment and decking are quickly covered in a thick blanket of white snow. Waves roll languidly, topping six feet in height but not steep enough to make more than an exaggerated rocking motion. A light wind blows and carries the flakes on the air currents, visible in the occasional moonlight. (Temp H 33/1 L 26/–3, Wind — 5–10 mph. Characters moving on deck must succeed on a saving throw each round or be knocked prone. All exposed areas of the ship are lightly obscured.)

01–20	Clear blue sky overhead provides ample room for the bright sun to shine. Wind gusts from the northeast, flapping the sail and nettings. Whitecapped waves topping seven to eight feet high seem to be pushing large chunks of ice along in their grasp. (Temp H 30/–1 L –26/–3, Wind — 10–15 mph. Those working while facing the sun must succeed on a DC 10 Constitution saving throw or be blinded for 1d4 hours. Characters with a natural sensitivity to light take a –1 penalty to the saving throw. There is a 10% chance of a course changed being required for an ice floe in the path of the ship.)
21–40	Sun and gray clouds do battle overhead for power, sometimes plunging the water into a dark twilight or bright daylight. Numerous waves about the size of a man run the length of the water as far as the eye can see, all topped with a cone of blue-white froth. The wind picks this froth from each and carries it along, freezing it to any surface it covers. The rigging and sails labor under the extra weight of the ice, glinting like jewels in the periodic sun. (Temp H 29/–2 L 21/–6, Wind — 20–25 mph. Characters moving on deck must succeed on a saving throw each round or be knocked prone. There is a 12% chance of a course change being required for an ice floe in the path of the ship.)
41–60	A wide bank of clouds blots out the sun; consequently, the diluted light colors the world in tints of twilight gray. The absence of wind allows the sails and rigging to hang listless, like cloth in a shop window. The water is unmarked, calm for many miles around the ship, with waves visible in the far distance. Pressure seems to build, raising the temperature over several hours to a more comfortable level. Icebergs in the distance hold steady like islands. (Temp H 32/0 L 28/–2, Wind — 0–5 mph. Experienced sailors know a storm is coming. Reroll on Arctic day–rain chart in 1d4 hours for result. There is a 2% chance of a course change being required for icebergs in the path of the ship.)
61–80	Streamers of billowy clouds race overhead in the wind. Large waves buffet the ship, attempting to carry it along with them. Wind assaults the vessel hard from the west, never wavering or letting up. Tacking into the wind seems impossible from its vicious force while tacking with the wind runs a risk of never getting back control of the ship. (Temp H 23/–5 L 18/–8, Wind — 25–35 mph.)
81–00	The air burns with the wind chill crusting ice all over the ship, the sun adding no aid to the frigid temperature. Clouds are nonexistent in the sky, collecting only on the horizons. While filling the sails, the wind steals the breath from those on deck and freezes exposed flesh in minutes. (Temp H 22/–5 L 15/–10, Wind — 35–40 mph. Characters moving on deck must succeed on a saving throw each round or be knocked prone.)

01–20	Clear ebony sky overhead provides astronomers and navigators a fine view of the stars and planets. A gentle wind blows from the south, flapping the sail and nettings. Small waves lap against the side of the boat like a heartbeat; icebergs stand out stark white against the black background of the water and night sky. (Temp H 32/0 L 25/–4, Wind — 5–10 mph. There is a 2% chance of course changes being required for an ice floe in the path of the ship.)
21–40	Large clouds move overhead, blocking the stars and moon with their bulk. The ship rolls gently on the waves as it rides through the water. Occasionally, larger waves provide a small drop for the vessel as it is carried over the lip of the wave. The strong wind takes the ship along with it, filling the sails and pulling at cloaks of those on board. (Temp H 29/–2 L 24/–4, Wind — 10–15 mph.)
41–60	Clouds block all stars and only hint at the location of the moon, adding a claustrophobic feel to the trip. The absence of wind allows the sails and rigging to hang listless, like cloth in a shop window. The ebony water ripples in the soft breeze, with whitecaps standing out like glowing embers. (Temp H 31/0 L 26/–3, Wind — 0–5 mph. There is a 2% chance of a course change being required for icebergs in the path of the ship).
61–80	Partial clouds covers sections of the sky, seemingly unmoving. Large waves buffet the ship, attempting to carry it along with them. Wind assaults the vessel hard from the west, never wavering or letting up. Travel during the night at full sail run a double risk of colliding with ice. (Temp H 30/–1 L 22/–5, Wind — 25–35 mph. There is a 15% chance of a course change being required for ice).
81–00	Wisps of cloud move across the sky, sometimes blocking the stars. The brightness of the visible stars and moon provides ample light to maneuver around the ship and perform most tasks. The ever-present wind provides enough force to keep the ship moving at optimum speed. The absence of spray from the calm waters allows for equipment to dry. (Temp H 30/–1 L 26/–3, Wind — 10–15 mph.)

EQUATORIAL

Within the Equatorial region, humidity is an issue for temperature measurement. Reference the Humidity Table to bring about a more realistic gauge for temperature; consequently, the effects of heat upon those traveling the waves should be watched closely.

01–20	A strong wind blows, adding a texture to the warm rain falling. The occasional rain mists on the warm deck, adding more humidity to the air. A sticky aspect of the air grows throughout the day as the humidity rises. Bright sun reflects off all wet and shiny surfaces, creating a glare from all directions. Waves are large in width but not in height, rocking the ship with their passage. (Temp H 79/27 L 65/19, Wind — 10–15 mph.)
21–40	Heavy rain pummels the ship and those on board, drenching all equipment and passengers. The waves are sedate, rarely topping eight feet, seemingly held down with the impact of the rain. The sun tries to pierce the cloud cover with its intense glare, only succeeding in raising the temperature. Wind is nonexistent and hammered to submission by the heavy rain. (Temp H 75/24 L 71/22, Wind — 0–5 mph.)
41–60	Seemingly in rhythm with the lapping waves, periodic rain drops in vast amounts, quickly soaking all surfaces and washing away loose items. Between rainfalls, the sun attempts to burn away the moisture with blistering heat but is never quite successful, and so leaves all with a heaviness of moisture. Waves roll languidly, topping six feet in height but not steep enough to make more than an exaggerated rocking motion. The wind blows merrily, billowing out the sails of the ship and propelling the vessel over the large waves. (Temp H 79/27 L 71/22, Wind — 20–25 mph. Characters moving on deck during a deluge must succeed on a saving throw each round or be knocked prone and pushed five feet in a random direction.)
61–80	A drizzle of rain, sporadically hard and light, falls throughout the day. All surfaces are thoroughly soaked and heavy with water. The warmth of the occasional sun is diminished slightly by the cool rain, keeping it tolerable for all involved. The wind blows constantly, keeping the sails full but not pushing the limit of its capabilities. (Temp H 81/28 L 77/26, Wind — 25–30 mph.)

81–00	Heavy rain from unseen clouds pummels the ship and those on deck. Waves like great green battering rams smash against the ship every minute. The overhead clouds descend to a point where it seems the ship is in a large chamber. Wind hurtles against the vessel and its sail, trying to rip it free from the mast and rigging. All loose items are tossed around the decking to create hazards for those on deck. (Temp H 80/27 L 74/24, Wind — 25–30 mph. Characters moving on deck must succeed on a saving throw each round or be knocked prone and pushed five feet in a random direction.)

Rain/Night

01–20	The humidity of the night is made comfortable by the patter of rain upon the deck. The coolness of the rain seems to steal some of the thickness in the air. The thin clouds mask the presence of the stars but leave a large halo where the moon tries to shine. The waves crash against the hull as if trying to keep the ship from reaching its goal. The bounce of the ship as it passes over the waves keeps all but the soundest sleepers awake. (Temp H 80/27 L 70/22, Wind — 0–5 mph.)
21–40	Heavy rain from ebony clouds press down on the ship and those on deck. Waves can be seen in the dark like great gray-green boulders that smash against the ship every minute. The overhead clouds descend to a point where it seems the ship is in a large chamber. Wind hurtles against the vessel and its sail, trying to rip it from the mast and rigging. All loose items and small creatures on deck vie for attention from the crashing waves or the blustery wind. (Temp H 77/26 L 62/17, Wind — 20–25 mph. Characters moving on deck must succeed on a saving throw each round or be knocked prone. All exposed areas of the ship are lightly obscured.)
41–60	Seemingly in rhythm with the lapping waves, periodic rain drops in vast amounts, quickly soaking all surfaces and washing away loose materials. Waves roll languidly, topping six feet in height but not steep enough to make more than an exaggerated rocking motion. A light wind blows carrying a humid mist from the still warm water, visible in the intermittent moonlight. (Temp H 76/25 L 71/22, Wind — 5–10 mph. Characters moving on deck must succeed on a saving throw each round or be knocked prone. All exposed areas of the ship are lightly obscured.)
61–80	A drizzle of rain, sometimes hard and sometimes light, falls continuously throughout during the nighttime hours. All surfaces are thoroughly soaked and heavy with water. The warmth of the day rapidly disappears replaced with the humidity of the still evaporating water around the ship. The waves are smaller than normal and works with the rain to stay weak enough to be inconsequential. The wind blows constantly, keeping the sails full but not pushing the limit of its capabilities. (Temp H 80/27 L 78/26, Wind — 312–18 mph.)
81–00	A thrashing rain accompanies hurricane force winds. In the distance amid lightning flashes, waterspouts can be seen reaching for the sky. Waves the size of small mountains rise above the vessel, giving the ship a wide span of view when atop a wave and a sense of claustrophobia when in a gully. (Temp H 79/27 L 71/22, Wind — 80–85 mph. Characters moving on deck must succeed on a saving throw with a –1 penalty each round or be knocked prone and pushed 15 feet in a random direction. All exposed areas of the ship are lightly obscured.)

Dry/Day

01–20	The incessant sun is offset by a breeze, keeping the temperature to a seemingly more moderate level. Spray flies up in the wind, fed by the many whitecapped waves sprinting past the ship. The horizon is marked with a large bank of gray clouds, promising rain in the next day or two. The humidity rises throughout the day, adding a weight to the sun that saps the strength of those not acquainted with the equatorial waters. (Temp H 81/28 L 75/24, Wind — 20–25 mph.)
21–40	Clouds run amok along the sky, occasionally blocking the sun and its warmth. The wind seemingly growls as it tears across the water at the ship. The sail quivers, trying to keep the wind from escaping. Waves rise up and crash against the hull of the ship, each impact like a bludgeon from nature itself. (Temp H 77/26 L 69/21, Wind — 25–35 mph.)
41–60	A crystal clear sky magnifies the sun, aiming its heat against the ship and her crew. The wind puffs slowly, not enough to cool the flesh of those in the open or ruffle the sails. Waves move across the water like a herd, trying to carry the ship along in their wake, fighting the vessel should it try to turn away. The spray carries over the rail into the faces of those on deck, quickly drying to leave powdered salt. (Temp H 77/26 L 65/19, Wind — 0–5 mph.)
61–80	The thick clouds overhead threaten to release their load, moisture currently released in the form of a thick palpable air. While no rain has fallen during the day, all surfaces are beaded with sweat and spray from the humidity-laced air. The moderate wind moves both the ship and the clouds, lifting the waves to heights of 10 feet, launching the spray into the air. The ship rolls with the impacts as it tips down one wave and up another, the prow having difficulty cutting through the water. (Temp H 77/26 L 70/22, Wind — 25–30 mph.)
81–00	The sky is clear, dotted with the occasional cloud. A steady wind blows determined to cart items away in its embrace. The weak sun cannot raise the temperature, regardless of its steady glare. Abundant waves run to the horizon, making up for size with numbers. The water is churned to a gray-green, and you can see only a few feet under the surface with any clarity, another indicator of the weak sun. (Temp H 75/25 L 64/18, Wind — 35–40 mph.)

Dry/Night

01–20	Clear sky provides a view of the numerous constellations and guiding stars. Wind gusts from the northeast, creating a flapping staccato to match the waves breaking on the hull of the ship. Whitecapped waves, visible in the moonlight, reach for the sailors on board, topping seven to eight feet. A slight mist can be felt in the wind; consequently, all surfaces are slick and shiny with moisture. (Temp H 75/25 L 61/17, Wind — 15–25 mph.)
21–40	Clouds of stone gray run from horizon to horizon, extinguishing the stars and moon from view. The absence of wind allows the sails and rigging to hang listless, like cloth in a shop window. The water is calm for many miles around the ship, with waves visible in the far distance. Pressure seems to build, raising the temperature over several hours to just above a comfortable level. (Temp H 76/25 L 63/18, Wind — 0–5 mph. Experienced sailors know a storm is coming. Reroll on Equatorial day-rain chart in 1d4 hours for result.)
41–60	The cool of the night is identified by the daytime heat escaping the decking, misting the moisture collected through the daylight hours. Besides raising the humidity to an uncomfortable level, it also deadens the night sounds of the creaking riggings and lapping waves. Long trenches of waves roll the ship as it moves through them like long strides of a great beast. Occasional clouds plunge the world into darkness, allowing the moon and stars to peer through again in a few moments. (Temp H 74/24 L 69/21, Wind — 10–20 mph.)
61–80	Lines of clouds run the length of the night sky. The bright moon hides behind this occasional cover, sometimes plunging the world into a dark twilight or bright moonlight. Numerous waves about the size of a man run the length of the water as far as the eye can see, all topped with a cone of greenish-white froth. The rigging and sails have rivulets of collected water that pools on the deck. Lines are heavy with water and deck boards are slick and shiny, sometimes reflecting the occasional sunlight. (Temp H 78/26 75/24, Wind — 20–25 mph.)

| 81–00 | Clear ebony night overhead provides astronomers and navigators a fine view of the stars and planets. A gentle wind blows from the west, flapping the sail and nettings. Small waves lap against the side of the boat like a heartbeat; reflections of the moon on the waves stand out stark white against the black background of the water and night sky. (Temp H 79/27 L 67/20, Wind — 5–10 mph.) |

WINTER

TROPICAL

RAIN/DAY

01–20	A gentle breeze blows, adding a pleasant cooling to the warm rain falling. Large drops patter along the deck, but quickly evaporate and add to the humidity. A sticky aspect of the air grows throughout the day as the humidity rises. Sunlight glints off the water like numerous smaller suns, blinding those not ready for the effect. Waves are large in width but not in height and rock the ship with their passage. (Temp H 88/32 L 75/25, Wind — 10–15 mph.)
21–40	Steady rainfall descends upon the ship and those on board, quickly soaking all equipment and people. The waves are sedate, rarely topping five feet and seemingly held down with the rain. The sun tries to pierce the cloud cover with its intense glare, but only succeeds in raising the temperature. Wind is nonexistent, hammered to submission by the heavy rain (Temp H 83/29 L 78/26, Wind — 0–5 mph.)
41–60	Waves brush against the ship in counterpoint to the periodic rain, which falls in vast amounts, quickly waterlogging everything. Between rainfalls, the sun attempts to burn away the moisture with blistering heat. Waves roll, languidly topping six feet in height but not steep enough to make more than an exaggerated rocking motion. The wind blows merrily, billowing out the sails of the ship and propelling the vessel over the large waves. (Temp H 89/23 L 76/ 25, Wind — 20–25 mph. Characters moving on deck must succeed on a saving throw each round or be knocked prone and pushed 10 feet in a random direction.)
61–80	Rain falls continuously through the day, varying between hard and soft, keeping all items and surfaces heavy with moisture. The warmth of the occasional sun is diminished slightly by the cool rain, keeping it tolerable for all involved. The wind blows constantly, keeping the sails full but not pushing the limit of its capabilities. (Temp H 83/29 L 70/22, Wind — 25–30 mph.)
81–00	Blankets of water fall from the sky, creating a deluge that threatens to wash away all on deck. Waves like great gray-green boulders smash against the ship every minute. The overhead clouds descend to a point where it seems the ship is in a large chamber. Wind hurtles against the vessel and its sail, trying to rip it from the mast and rigging. (Temp H 87/32 L 74/24, Wind — 20–25 mph. Characters moving on deck must succeed on a saving throw each round or be knocked prone and pushed 10 feet in a random direction. All exposed areas of the ship are lightly obscured.)

RAIN/NIGHT

01–20	While cool, the night remains uncomfortable due to the humidity carried on the air. The moon makes itself known through the clouds, illuminating a portion of the night sky to milky white. The waves crash against the hull as if trying to keep the ship from reaching its goal. The bounce of the ship as it passes over the waves keeps all but the soundest sleepers awake. (Temp H 86/31 L 79/27, Wind — 0–5 mph.)
21–40	Heavy rain from substantial clouds pummel the ship and those on deck. Waves can be seen in the dark like great gray-green boulders that smash against the ship every minute. The overhead clouds descend to a point where it seems the ship is in a large chamber. Wind hurtles against the vessel and its sail, trying to rip it from the mast and rigging. All loose items and small creatures on deck vie for attention from the crashing waves or the blustery wind. (Temp H 85/30 L 79/27, Wind — 50–55 mph. Characters moving on deck must succeed on a saving throw each round or be knocked prone. All exposed areas of the ship are lightly obscured.)
41–60	Seemingly in rhythm with the lapping waves, periodic rain drops in vast amounts, quickly soaking all surfaces and washing away loose items. Waves roll languidly, topping six feet in height but not steep enough to make more than an exaggerated rocking motion. A light wind blows, carrying mist from the still warm water that is visible in the occasional moonlight. (Temp H 87/31 L 77/26, Wind — 5–10 mph. All exposed areas of the ship are lightly obscured.)
61–80	A drizzle of rain falls endlessly during the nighttime hours. All surfaces are thoroughly soaked and heavy with water. The warmth of the day rapidly disappears, replaced with the humidity of the still-evaporating water around the ship. Waves are present but pose no real threat to the direction of the ship or her course. The wind blows constantly, keeping the sails full but not pushing the limit of its capabilities. (Temp H 83/29 L 77/26, Wind — 12–18 mph.)
81–00	A constant rain falls from gray clouds overhead, keeping all within it thoroughly soaked. The wind propels the ship slowly, seemingly held back by the rain, over the large hillock-shaped waves. Occasional lightning flashes illuminate the depth of the rain, looking like iron bars for as far as the eye can see. (Temp H 79/27 L 71/22, Wind — 5–10 mph. All exposed areas of the ship are lightly obscured.)

DRY/DAY

01–20	The large sun dominates the sky but a swift breeze keeps the temperature to a more moderate level. Spray pulled up from the many waves, which are capped in white froth. The horizon is marked with a large bank of gray clouds and promise rain in the next day or two. (Temp H 85/30 L 72/23, Wind — 20–25 mph.)
21–40	Clouds run riot along the sky, occasionally blocking the sun and its warmth. The wind seemingly growls as it tears across the water at the ship. The sail quivers, trying to keep the wind from escaping. Waves rise up and crash against the hull of the ship, with each impact like a bludgeon from nature itself. (Temp H 86/31 L 75/ 25, Wind — 25–35 mph.)
41–60	A crystal clear sky magnifies the sun and directs its heat against the ship and her crew. The wind puffs slowly, not enough to extinguish a candle let alone cool the flesh of those in the open. Waves move across the water like a herd, trying to carry the ship along in their wake, fighting the vessel should it try to turn away. The spray carries over the rail into the faces of those on deck, quickly drying to leave powdered salt. (Temp H 84/29 L 77/26, Wind — 0–5 mph.)
61–80	The thick clouds overhead threaten to release their burden but maintain their hold for now. The moderate wind moves both the ship and the clouds, lifting the waves to heights of 10 feet and launching the spray into the air. The ship rolls with the impacts as it tips down one wave and up another, the prow having difficulty cutting through the water. (Temp H 89/32 L 82/29, Wind — 25–30 mph.)

81–00	The sky is clear, dotted with numerous small mediocre puffs of cloud. A steady wind blows and seems determined to cart items away in its embrace. The sun high overhead seems at a greater distance than usual given the lack of heat generated. Abundant waves run to the horizon, making up for size with numbers. The water is churned to a gray-green, and you can see only a few feet under the surface with any clarity, another indicator of the weak sun. (Temp H 88/32 L 80/28, Wind — 20–25 mph.)

Dry/Night

01–20	Clear sky provides a view of the innumerable constellations and guiding stars. Wind gusts from the south and create a flapping staccato to match the waves breaking on the hull of the ship. Whitecapped waves, visible in the moonlight, reach for the sailors on board and top 10 feet. A slight mist can be felt in the wind; consequently, all surfaces are slick and shiny with moisture. (Temp H 87/31 L 81/28, Wind — 30–35 mph.)
21–40	Clouds of dull steel run from horizon to horizon, extinguishing the stars and moon from view. The lack of wind allows the sails and rigging to hang listless, like cloth in a shop window. The water is unmarked, tranquil for many miles around the ship, with waves visible in the far distance. Pressure seems to build, raising the temperature over several hours to just above a comfortable level. (Temp H 86/31 L 80/28, Wind — 0–5 mph. Experienced sailors know a storm is coming. Reroll on Tropical day-rain chart in 1d4 hours for result.)
41–60	The cool of the night is acknowledged by the daytime heat escaping the decking, misting the moisture collected through the daylight hours. Besides raising the humidity to an uncomfortable level, it also deadens the night sounds of creaking riggings and lapping waves. Troughs of water roll the ship as it moves through them like long strides of a great beast. Occasional clouds steal the minimal light and allow the moon and stars to peer through again in a few moments. (Temp H 90/33 L 84/29, Wind — 10–20 mph.)
61–80	The clouds battle with the moon overhead for supremacy, plunging the world into pitch dark or muted twilight. Numerous waves about the size of a man run the length of the water as far as the eye can see, all topped with a cone of greenish-white froth. The rigging and sails have rivulets of collected water that pools on the deck. Lines are heavy with water and deck boards are slick and shiny, sometimes reflecting the occasional moonlight. (Temp H 83/29 L 74/24, Wind — 20–25 mph.)
81–00	Clear ebony night overhead provides astronomers and navigators a fine view of the stars and planets. A gentle wind blows from the west flaps the sail and nettings. Small waves lap against the side of the boat like a heartbeat, and reflections of the moon on the waves stand out stark white against the black background of the water and night sky. (Temp H 83/29 L 78/26, Wind — 10–15 mph.)

Temperate

Rain/Day

01–20	A gentle breeze blows, adding a slight chill to the damp air. Large drops patter along the deck, but are warmed by the periodic sun and quickly evaporate. Gray-white clouds fill the sky from horizon to horizon, predicting a constant rainfall. Waves are large in width but not in height and rock the ship with their passage (Temp H 46/9 L 35/2, Wind — 5–10 mph.)
21–40	Rain from onyx clouds thrash the ship and those unfortunate enough to be on deck. Waves like great gray-green behemoths smash against the ship every few minutes. The overhead clouds descend and gather the ship in its embrace. Wind hurtles against the vessel and its sail, trying to rip it from the mast and rigging. The clouds of mist streak by on the fierce wind, presenting the illusion of even greater speed. All loose items on deck vie for attention from the crashing waves or the blustery wind. (Temp H 54/13 L 42/6, Wind — 55–60 mph. Characters moving on deck must succeed on a saving throw each round or be knocked prone. All exposed areas of the ship are lightly obscured.)

41–60	The sky carries a darker shade than normal, with clouds so thick they block out all trace of light. Rain is propelled horizontally with the wind, hitting like daggers and needles and reducing vision to mere feet around each person. Winds blow loose objects and people unprepared for its force off course. Waves 15–30 feet high assault the ship, blowing over the rail and soaking sailors with its frigid embrace. (Temp H 44/8 L 37/3, Wind — 40–45 mph NE. Characters moving on deck must succeed on a saving throw each round or be knocked prone and pushed five feet in a random direction. All exposed areas of the ship are lightly obscured.)
61–80	A constant rain falls from gray clouds overhead, keeping all within it thoroughly soaked. The wind propels the ship slowly, seemingly held back by the rain, over the large hillock-shaped waves. Occasional lightning flashes illuminate the depth of the rain, looking like iron bars for as far as the eye can see. (Temp H 50/11 L 40/5, Wind — 5–10 mph NE. All exposed areas of the ship are lightly obscured.)
81–00	A simple rain falls and creates a constant drone of rain on the wooden deck. The wind is not strong enough to alter the vertical direction of the rain and lets the sail hang like a soaked rag from the mast. The subtle waves rock the ship almost undetectably as they move by on unseen currents. Clouds looking like an inverted mountain range press down upon the ship and crew. (Temp H 44/8 L 33/1, Wind — 10–15 mph.)

Rain/Night

01–20	Clouds brimming with lightning streak by overhead as waves lift like cliffs (six to 15 feet) around the vessel. Rain alternates from side-to-side and straight down with the force of a hammer blow. Rivers of water course around the deck from the rain, and waves create treacherous footing for all on board. The sails snap and crack as it fills with the wind, dropping deluges of collected rain to the deck below. Periodically, the sky lights up with a nearby lightning blast, painting everything in shades of white, blue, and gray; all other times, the charcoal sky and water bestow a sense of isolation. (Temp H 47/9 L 41/6, Wind — 20–25 mph. Characters moving on deck must succeed on a saving throw each round or be knocked prone and pushed five feet in a random direction. All exposed areas of the ship are lightly obscured.)
21–40	A constant rain falls from gray clouds overhead, keeping all within it thoroughly soaked. The wind propels the ship slowly, seemingly held back by the rain, over the large hillock-shaped waves. Occasional lightning flashes illuminate the depth of the rain, looking like iron bars for as far as the eye can see. (Temp H 45/8 L 38/4, Wind — 5–10 mph. All exposed areas of the ship are lightly obscured.)
41–60	Thick rolling clouds erupt constantly with thunder, and rain beats upon the wooden planks. The percussion of the rain is accented with the occasional spray of mountainous waves carried on the wind. Gusts of wind blow across the ship and attempt to pull everything along in its wake. Sight is reduced to feet, the distance eliminated with the thick sheets of rain. (Temp H 50/11 L 43/7, Wind — 15–20 mph. Characters moving on deck must succeed on a saving throw each round or be knocked prone. All exposed areas of the ship are heavily obscured.)
61–80	Hurricane force rain and wind toss the ship like a child's doll. Huge waves like mountains threaten to topple the vessel and launch the sailors into the unforgiving sea. Wind blows fiercely, lifting all heavy objects not lashed down and propelling them around and off the ship. The sky and water are undistinguishable, erasing the horizon as both are steel gray. (Temp H 39/4 L 31/0, Wind — 75–80 mph NNW. Characters moving on deck must succeed on a saving throw with a –1 penalty each round or be knocked prone and pushed 15 feet in a random direction.)

| 81–00 | A simple rain falls and creates a constant drone of rain on the wooden deck. The wind is not strong enough to alter the vertical direction of the rain and lets the sail hang like a soaked rag from the mast. The faint waves rock the ship almost indiscernibly as they move on underwater currents. Clouds looking like an inverted mountain range press down upon the ship and crew. Navigation can be done only through compass or landmarks. (Temp H 60/16 L 52/12, Wind — 5–10 mph E.) |

Dry/Day

01–20	The large sun governs the sky but a swift breeze keeps the temperature to a cooler level. Spray pulled up from the many waves, each capped in white froth, is thrown across the deck. The horizon is marked with a large bank of gray clouds promising rain in the next day or two. (Temp H 56/14 L 44/8, Wind — 20–25 mph.)
21–40	The sky is clear and dotted with numerous small unimposing puffs of cloud. A steady wind blows and seems determined to cart items away in its embrace. The sun high overhead seems at a greater distance than usual given the lack of heat generated. Abundant waves run to the horizon, making up for size with numbers. The water is churned to a gray-green, and you can see only a few feet under the surface with any clarity, another indicator of the weak sun. (Temp H 58/15 L 49/10, Wind — 15–20 mph.)
41–60	A crystal clear sky magnifies the sun and directs its heat against the ship and her crew. The wind puffs slowly, not enough to extinguish a candle let alone cool the flesh of those warmer than usual day. Waves move across the water like a herd, trying to carry the ship along in their wake, fighting the vessel should it try to turn away. The spray carries over the rail into the faces of those on deck, quickly drying to leave crystals of powdered salt. (Temp H 60/16 L 52/12, Wind — 5–10 mph. Sunstroke in 3d8 rounds unless properly attired for the sun. Sunburn may be a risk.)
61–80	Sun and gray clouds do battle overhead for dominance, sometimes plunging the water into a dark twilight or bright daylight. Numerous waves about the size of a man run the length of the water as far as the eye can see, all topped with a cone of white froth. The wind picks this froth from each wave and carries it along and coats all surfaces. This cooling spray makes the trip enjoyable for most on board, even in the shade. The rigging and sails flap in the breeze, occasionally dropping additional sprays to the deck, glinting like jewels in the periodic sun. (Temp H 45/8 L 36/3, Wind — 18–20 mph N.)
81–00	Gray the color of stone has been painted from horizon to horizon, plunging the day into twilight. The absence of wind allows the sails and rigging to hang listless, like cloth in a shop window. The water is unmarked, calm for many miles around the ship, with waves visible in the far distance. Pressure seems to build, raising the temperature over several hours to a more comfortable level. (Temp H 55/13 L 46/9, Wind — 5–10 mph. Reroll in four game hours on the wet-day chart for the approaching storm.)

Dry/Night

| 01–20 | Clear sky provides a view of the numerous constellations and guiding stars. Wind gusts from the west, creating a flapping staccato to match the waves breaking on the hull of the ship. Whitecapped waves visible in the moonlight reach for the sailors on board, topping seven to eight feet. A slight mist can be felt in the wind; consequently, all surfaces are slick and shiny with moisture (Temp H 39/5 L 32/0, Wind — 15–25 mph.) |
| 21–40 | Clear jet-black night overhead provides astronomers and navigators a fine view of the stars and planets. A gentle wind blows from the south, flapping the sail and nettings. Small waves lap against the side of the boat like a heartbeat; small whitecaps stand out stark against the black background of the water and night sky. (Temp H 58/15 L 44/8, Wind — 15–25 mph.) |

41–60	An overcast sky blocks the view of all but the brightest stars and planets. Some navigation can still be done by experienced sailors. A breeze comes and goes, proving to be a fickle asset for the sails on the ship, waves playing tag gently rock the ship back and forth. (Temp H 49/10 L 43/7, Wind — 15–20 mph.)
61–80	Numerous stars turn the night sky into a twilight gray, offsetting the onyx of the calm water. A steady soft wind blows and propels the ship along on its way. The sound of the surf being cut by the hull is seemingly alone, periodically joined by the creak of the rigging and the soft voice of a sailor. (Temp H 55/13 L 44/8, Wind — 20–25 mph.)
81–00	A severe wind blows, threatening to rip the sail from the mast as it propels the vessel over the waves like a toy. Thick ribbons of cloud race overhead like gray gashes in the constellations. Many large waves run the length of vision, occasionally growing to such a large size (45 feet) that they threaten to topple the ship like flotsam. (Temp H 52/12 L 45/8, Wind 15–25 mph.)

Arctic

Wind chill is a real concern when the temperature drops below 32° F. Exposure to the wind risks frostbite for flesh. The effective temperature, for purposes of calculating potential harm caused by extreme cold, can be found in the Wind Chill Table.

Rain/Day

01–20	White-gray clouds span from horizon to horizon, and periodic deluges of snow drop upon the water and the ship. The deck is quickly covered in a white blanket of snow as it makes progress slow around the ship. Finding equipment is difficult for the inexperienced sailor, and boxes and barrels become nondescript objects in the snow. The wind moves the snow in various directions as it descends, moving the sails to half full with their strongest force. (Temp H –15/–26 L –20/–29, Wind — 15–20 mph.)
21–40	Sleet drops like sheets of needles upon sailors in the open. The wind drives the sleet almost horizontally across the waves. Large mountains of water move across the area and threaten to bash the vessel into submission. The steel-gray sky rolls like the underside of a surf promising many hours of attack. The rigging creaks and the sails moan ominously in the barrage of the storm. Movement along the deck is perilous at best; those in the upper reaches of the vessel cling for their lives. (Temp H –12/–25 L –23/–30, Wind — 20–25 mph. Characters moving on deck must succeed on a saving throw each round or be knocked prone. All exposed areas of the ship are lightly obscured.)
41–60	Freezing mist falls, landing like a blanket upon the water. Wind is present but too weak to fill the sails. Ice floes move on the sunken currents, dancing around the ship at great distances. Waves are subdued, seemingly moving in numerous directions with no discernible pattern. Ice forms on most surfaces with extended exposure, and sails and rigging become rigid and hazardous with each passing hour. (Temp H –14/–26 L –19/p–28, Wind — 0–5 mph. Characters moving on deck must succeed on a saving throw each round or be knocked prone. All exposed areas of the ship are lightly obscured.)
61–80	Clouds explode with lightning and thunder as waves lift like cliffs (six to 15 feet) around the vessel. Rain alternates from side-to-side and straight down with the force of a hammer blow. Ice coats all exposed surfaces in minutes and creates treacherous areas on the ship and rigging. The sails snap and crack as they fill with the wind, snow, and ice, dropping chunks of ice to the deck below. Periodically, the sky lights up with a nearby lightning blast that paints everything in shades of white and black; all other times, the charcoal sky and water bestow a sense of isolation. (Temp H –16/–27 L –25/–31, Wind — 25–35 mph. Characters moving on deck must succeed on a saving throw each round or be knocked prone. All exposed areas of the ship are lightly obscured.)

81–00 The sky carries a darker shade than normal, with clouds so thick they block out all trace of light. Rain is propelled horizontally with the wind, hitting like daggers and needles, and reducing vision to mere feet around each person. Ice forms on all surfaces and makes passage difficult on deck. Winds blow loose objects and people unprepared for its force off course. Waves 15–30 feet high assault the ship, blowing over the rail and soaking sailors with its frigid embrace. (Temp: H –20/–29 L –25/–31 Wind 40–45 mph. Characters moving on deck must succeed on a saving throw each round or be knocked prone and pushed five feet in a random direction. All exposed areas of the ship are heavily obscured.)

Rain/Night

01–20 Bulbous clouds promise a tremendous stormfront. Waves lift like cliffs (20–30 feet) around the vessel as rain attacks side-to-side and straight down with the force of a hammer blow. Ice coats all exposed surfaces in minutes, creating treacherous areas on the ship and rigging. The sails snap and crack as they fill with the wind, snow, and ice, dropping chunks of ice to the deck below. Periodically, the sky lights up with a nearby lightning blast that paints everything in shades of white; all other times, the charcoal sky and water bestow a sense of isolation. (Temp H –17/–27 L –24/–31, Wind — 25–35 mph. Characters moving on deck must succeed on a saving throw each round or be knocked prone and pushed five feet in a random direction. All exposed areas of the ship are lightly obscured. There is a 10% chance of a course change being required for ice formation in the path of the ship.)

21–40 Freezing mist falls like a cloud landing on the water. Wind is present but too weak to fill the sails. Ice floes move on the sunken currents, dancing around the ship at great distances. Waves are subdued and seemingly move in numerous directions with no discernible pattern. Ice forms on most surfaces with extended exposure, and sails and rigging become rigid and hazardous with each passing hour. (Temp H –18/–28 L –22/–30, Wind — 0–5 mph. Characters moving on deck must succeed on a saving throw each round or be knocked prone.)

41–60 The night sky carries a shade darker than normal, clouds so thick they block out all trace of light. Rain is propelled horizontally with the wind, hitting like daggers and needles, reducing vision to mere feet around each person. Ice forms on all surfaces and makes passage dangerous on deck and in the lines above. Winds blow loose objects and people unprepared for its force off course. Waves 15–30 feet high assault the ship, blowing over the rail and soaking sailors with its frigid embrace. (Temp H –16/–27 L –18/–28, Wind — 40–45 mph. Characters moving on deck must succeed on a saving throw each round or be knocked prone and pushed 10 feet in a random direction. All exposed areas of the ship are heavily obscured.)

61–80 Constant icy drizzle settles on all surfaces, turning the dark night into a dark gray, reducing vision to nearly nonexistent. Frigid temperatures freeze the moisture within minutes on every surface. Travel across deck is difficult but manageable to those familiar with their surroundings. Sound is subdued with the ice pellets, adding a muffling effect to conversations. Waves are unseen but can be felt hitting the ship every few seconds, occasionally bathing the deck with its spray, a testament to its height of several feet. (Temp H –15/–26 L –20/–29, Wind — 5–10 mph. Characters moving on deck must succeed on a saving throw each round or be knocked prone and pushed 10 feet in a random direction. All exposed areas of the ship are lightly obscured.)

81–00 Large thick flakes drop around the ship, landing softly on the water before melting. Equipment and decking are quickly covered in a thick blanket of white snow. Waves roll languidly, topping six feet in height but not steep enough to make more than an exaggerated rocking motion. A light wind blows and carries the flakes on the air currents, which are visible in the occasional moonlight. (Temp H –11/–24 L –19/–28, Wind — 5–10 mph. Characters moving on deck must succeed on a saving throw each round or be knocked prone. All exposed areas of the ship are lightly obscured.)

Dry/Day

01–20 Clear blue sky overhead provides ample room for the bright sun to shine. Wind gusts from the west, flapping the sail and nettings. Whitecapped waves topping seven to eight feet high seem to be pushing large chunks of ice along in their grasp. (Temp H –12/–25 L –17/–27, Wind — 10–15 mph. Those working while facing the sun must succeed on a saving throw or be blinded for 1d4 hours. Characters with a natural sensitivity to light take a –1 penalty on this saving throw. There is a 10% chance of a course changed being required for an ice flow in the path of the ship.)

21–40 Sun and gray clouds do battle overhead for power, sometimes plunging the water into a dark twilight or bright daylight. Numerous waves about the size of a man run the length of the water as far as the eye can see, all topped with a cone of white froth. The wind picks this froth from each and carries it along and freezes it to any surface it covers. The rigging and sails labor under the extra weight of the ice, glinting like jewels in the periodic sun. (Temp H –16/–27 L –22/–30, Wind — 20–25 mph. Characters moving on deck must succeed on a saving throw each round or be knocked prone. There is a 12% chance of a course change being required for an ice flow in the path of the ship.)

41–60 Gray the color of stone has been painted from horizon to horizon, plunging the day into twilight. The absence of wind allows the sails and rigging to hang listless, like cloth in a shop window. The water is unmarked, calm for many miles around the ship, with waves visible in the far distance. Pressure seems to build, raising the temperature over several hours to a more comfortable level. Icebergs in the distance hold steady like islands. (Temp H –17/–27 L –26/–32, Wind — 0–5 mph. Experienced sailors know a storm is coming. Reroll on Arctic day–rain chart in 1d4 hours for result. There is a 2% chance of a course change being required for icebergs in the path of the ship).

61–80 Streamers of billowy clouds race overhead in the wind. Large waves buffet the ship and attempt to carry it along with them. Wind assaults the vessel hard from the west, never wavering or letting up. Tacking into the wind seems impossible from its vicious force, while tacking with the wind runs a risk of never getting back control of the ship. (Temp H –19/–28 L –25/–31, Wind — 30–35 mph. Characters on the windward side of deck take a –1 penalty to saving throws.)

81–00 The air burns with the wind chill crusting ice all over the ship, with the sun adding no aid to the frigid temperature. Clouds are nonexistent in the sky, collecting only on the horizons. While filling the sails, the wind steals the breath from those on deck and freezes exposed flesh in minutes. (Temp H –18/–28 L –23/–30, Wind — 25–30 mph. Characters moving on deck must succeed on a saving throw each round or be knocked prone.)

Dry/Night

01–20 Untouched sky overhead provides astronomers and navigators a fine view of the stars and planets. A gentle wind blows from the south, flapping the sail and nettings. Small waves lap against the side of the boat like a heartbeat, and icebergs stand out stark white against the black background of the water and night sky. (Temp H –20/–29 L –25/ –32, Wind — 5–10 mph. There is a 10% chance of a course change being required for an ice floe in the path of the ship.)

21–40	Large clouds move overhead, blocking the stars and moon with their bulk. The ship rolls gently on the waves as it rides through the water. Occasionally larger waves provide a small drop for the vessel as it is carried over the lip of the wave. The strong wind takes the ship along with it, filling the sails and pulling at the cloaks of those on board. (Temp H –13/ –21 L –21/ –30, Wind — 45–50 mph.)
41–60	Clouds block all stars and only hint at the location of the moon, adding a claustrophobic feel to the trip. The absence of wind allows the sails and rigging to hang listless, like cloth in a shop window. The ebony water ripples in the soft breeze, with whitecaps standing out like glowing embers. (Temp H –19/–28 L –25/–32, Wind — 0–5 mph. There is a 2% chance of a course change being required for icebergs in the path of the ship.)
61–80	Partial clouds cover sections of the sky, seemingly unmoving. Large waves buffet the ship and attempt to carry it along with them. Wind assaults the vessel hard from the west, never wavering or letting up. Travel during the night at full sail runs double the risk of colliding with ice. (Temp H –23/–30 L –29/–33, Wind — 55–60 mph. Characters on deck take a –1 penalty to saving throws. There is a 15% chance of a course change being required for ice.)
81–00	Wisps of cloud move across the sky and sometimes block the stars. The brightness of the visible stars and moon provides ample light to maneuver around the ship and perform most tasks. The ever-present wind provides enough force to keep the ship moving at optimum speed. The absence of spray from the calm waters allows for equipment to dry. (Temp H –19/–28 L –21/–29, Wind — 30–35 mph.)

EQUATORIAL

Within the equatorial region, humidity is an issue for temperature measurement. Reference the Humidity Table for a more realistic gauge for temperature; consequently, the effects of heat upon those traveling the waves should be watched closely.

RAIN/DAY

01–20	A fierce wind blows, adding a texture to the warm rain falling. Large drops patter along the deck, and occasional sunshine warms the deck and quickly evaporates the rain and adds to the humidity. A sticky aspect of the air grows throughout the day as the humidity rises. Sunlight glints off the water like numerous smaller suns, blinding those not ready for the effect. Waves are large in width but not in height, rocking the ship with their passage. (Temp H 73/22 L 65/18, Wind — 35–40 mph.)
21–40	Heavy rain pummels the ship and those on board, quickly soaking everything on deck. The waves are sedate, rarely topping five feet, seemingly held down with the impact of the rain. The sun tries to pierce the cloud cover with its intense glare, but only succeeds in raising the temperature. Wind is nonexistent, hammered into submission by the heavy rain. (Temp H 70/21 L 62/17, Wind — 0–5 mph.)
41–60	Seemingly in rhythm with the lapping waves, periodic rain drops in vast amounts, quickly soaking all on board and washing away loose items. Between rainfalls, the sun attempts to burn away the moisture with blistering heat, but is never quite successful and so leaves all with a heaviness of moisture. Waves roll languidly, topping six feet in height but not steep enough to make more than an exaggerated rocking motion. The wind blows merrily, billowing out the sails of the ship and propelling the vessel over the large waves. (Temp H 67/19 L 58/15, Wind — 10–15 mph. Characters moving on deck during a deluge must succeed on a saving throw each round or be knocked prone and pushed 10 feet in a random direction.)

61–80	A drizzle of rain, sometimes hard and sometimes light, falls throughout the day. All equipment is thoroughly soaked and heavy with water. The warmth of the occasional sun is diminished slightly by the cool rain, keeping it tolerable for all involved. The wind blows constantly, keeping the sails full but not pushing the limit of their capabilities. Waves rise from the water to knock the ship with thundering impacts every few minutes. (Temp H 73/22 L 66/19, Wind — 20–25 mph.)
81–00	Thick rains from gargantuan clouds clobber the ship and those on deck. Waves like great green battering rams smash against the ship every few minutes. The overhead clouds descend to a point where it seems the ship is in a large chamber. Wind hurtles against the vessel and its sail, trying to rip it free from the mast and rigging. All loose items are tossed around the decking, creating hazards for those on deck. (Temp H 67/19 L 59/15, Wind — 50–55 mph. Characters moving on deck must succeed on a saving throw each round or be knocked prone and pushed 10 feet in a random direction.)

RAIN/NIGHT

01–20	The humidity of the night is made comfortable by the patter of rain upon the deck, with the coolness of the rain stealing some of the heat. The thin clouds mask the presence of the stars but leave a large halo where the moon tries to shine. The waves crash against the hull as if trying to keep the ship from reaching its goal. The bounce of the ship as it passes over the waves keeps all but the soundest sleepers awake. (Temp H 74/24 L 64/18, Wind — 0–5 mph.)
21–40	A deluge of rain from ebony clouds presses down on the ship and those on deck. Waves can be seen in the dark like great gray-green boulders that smash against the ship every minute. The overhead clouds descend to a point where it seems the ship is in a large chamber. Wind hurtles against the vessel and its sail, trying to rip it from the mast and rigging. All loose items and small creatures on deck vie for attention from the crashing waves or the blustery wind. (Temp H 71/21 L 62/17, Wind — 45–50 mph.)
41–60	Seemingly in rhythm with the lapping waves, periodic rain drops in vast amounts, quickly soaking all surfaces and washing away loose materials. Waves roll languidly, topping six feet in height but not steep enough to make more than an exaggerated rocking motion. A light wind blows carrying a humid mist from the still warm water that is visible in the intermittent moonlight. (Temp H 75/24 L 66/19, Wind — 15–20 mph. Characters moving on deck during a deluge must succeed on a saving throw each round or be knocked prone and pushed 10 feet in a random direction. All exposed areas of the ship are lightly obscured.)
61–80	A drizzle of rain, flipflopping between hard and light, falls continuously throughout the nighttime hours. All surfaces are thoroughly soaked and heavy with water. The warmth of the day rapidly disappears and is replaced with the humidity of the still-evaporating water around the ship. The waves are smaller than normal and work with the rain to stay weak enough to be inconsequential. The wind blows constantly, keeping the sails full but not pushing the limit of their capabilities. (Temp H 78/25 L 71/21, Wind — 30–35 mph.)
81–00	A thrashing rain accompanies hurricane force winds. In the distance amid lightning flashes, waterspouts can be seen reaching for the sky. Waves the size of small mountains rise above the vessel and give the ship a wide span of view when atop a wave and a sense of claustrophobia when in a gully. (Temp H 72/22 L 68/20, Wind — 75–85 mph. Characters moving on deck must succeed on a saving throw with a –1 penalty each round or be knocked prone and pushed 15 feet in a random direction. All exposed areas of the ship are lightly obscured.)

01–20 The large sun dominates the sky but a swift breeze keeps the temperature to a more moderate level. Spray is pulled up from the many waves, which are capped in white froth. The horizon is marked with a large bank of gray clouds that promise rain in the next day or two. The humidity rises throughout the day, adding a weight to the sun that saps the strength of those not acquainted with the equatorial waters. (Temp H 79/26 L 72/22, Wind — 10–15 mph.)

21–40 Clouds run amok along the sky, occasionally blocking the sun and its warmth. The wind seemingly growls as it tears across the water at the ship. The sail quivers from trying to keep the wind from escaping. Waves rise up and crash against the hull of the ship, each impact like a bludgeon from nature itself. (Temp H 75/24 L 65/15, Wind — 45–50 mph.)

41–60 A crystal-clear sky allows the sun to direct its heat against the ship and her crew. The wind breathes slowly, not enough to extinguish a candle let alone cool the flesh of those in the open. Waves move across the water like a herd, trying to carry the ship along in their wake, fighting the vessel should it try to turn away. The spray carries over the rail into the faces of those on deck, quickly drying to leave powdered salt. (Temp H 74/24 L 69/20, Wind — 0–5 mph.)

61–80 The turbulent clouds overhead threaten to release their load, allowing the moisture to be released in the form of a thick palpable air. While no rain has fallen during the day, all surfaces are beaded with sweat and spray from the moisture-laced air. The moderate wind moves both the ship and the clouds, lifting the waves to heights of 10 feet, launching the spray into the air. The ship rolls with the impacts as it tips down one wave and up another, the prow having difficulty cutting through the water. (Temp H 68/20 L 60/10 Wind — 20–25 mph.)

81–00 The sky is clear, dotted with numerous small unimposing collections of cloud. A steady wind blows, determined to cart items away in its embrace. The sun high overhead seems at a greater distance than usual given the lack of heat generated. Abundant waves run to the horizon, making up for size with numbers. The water is churned to a gray-green, and you can see only a few feet under the surface with any clarity, another indicator of the weak sun. (Temp H 75/24 L 71/21, Wind — 20–25 mph.)

01–20 An open sky provides a view of the numerous constellations and guiding stars. Wind gusts from the northeast, creating a flapping staccato to match the waves breaking on the hull of the ship. Whitecapped waves, visible in the moonlight, reach for the sailors on board, topping seven to eight feet. A slight mist can be felt in the wind; consequently, all surfaces are slick and shiny with moisture. (Temp H 74/24 L 67/19, Wind — 20–35 mph.)

21–40 Clouds reminiscent of the underside of gray crashing surf run from horizon to horizon, extinguishing the stars and moon from view. The absence of wind allows the sails and rigging to hang listless, like cloth in a shop window. The water is like glass, calm for many miles around the ship, with waves visible in the far distance. Pressure seems to build, raising the temperature over several hours to just above a comfortable level. (Temp H 70/21 L 61/16, Wind — 0–5 mph. Experienced sailors know a storm is coming. Reroll on Equatorial day–rain chart in 1d4 hours for result.)

41–60 The cool of the night is identified by the daytime heat escaping the decking, misting the moisture collected through the daylight hours. Besides raising the humidity to an uncomfortable level, it also deadens the night sounds of the creaking riggings and lapping waves. Long trenches of waves roll the ship as it moves through them like long strides of a great beast. Occasional clouds plunge the world into darkness, allowing the moon and stars to peer through again in a few moments. (Temp H 76/25 L 69/21, Wind — 10–20 mph.)

61–80 Thin clouds attempt to block the bright moonlight, but only mute the brilliance periodically. Rain falls lightly from unseen sources and slowly drench the ship and equipment. Numerous waves about 10 feet tall run the length of the water as far as the eye can see, all topped with a cone of greenish-white froth. The rigging and sails have rivulets of collected water that pools on the deck. Lines are heavy with water and deck boards are slick and shiny, sometimes reflecting the occasional sunlight. (Temp H 62/17 58/15, Wind — 20–25 mph.)

81–00 A clear night overhead provides astronomers and navigators a fine view of the stars and planets. A gentle wind blows from the south, flapping the sail and nettings. Small waves lap against the side of the boat like a heartbeat, reflections of the moon on the waves stand out stark white against the black background of the water and night sky. (Temp H 67/19 L 61/16, Wind — 5–10 mph.)

CHAPTER 4: NEW SPELLS

Most of these new spells deal with water-related events, ships, sailing, the ocean, or the weather.

SPELL LISTS

CLERIC SPELLS

1st Level
Anchor
Control Fog
Detect Current
Detect Land
3rd Level
Cause Bends
4th Level
Farvision
Ironrope
5th Level
Land Sail

DRUID SPELLS

1st Level
Control Fog
Detect Current
Detect Fish
Detect Land
2nd Level
Ballast
Fill the Sails

Hard Water Weapon
Undertow
3rd Level
Cause Bends
Strangling Seaweed
4th Level
Lunar Glare
Stonehull
5th Level
Air Sphere
Create Iceberg
Split Ice
7th Level
Create Island

MAGIC-USER SPELLS

1st Level
Anchor
Buoyancy
Control Fog
Detect Current
Detect Fish
Detect Land
Unseen Pilot
2nd Level
Ballast
Boarding Plank

Fill the Sails
Hard Water Weapon
Spectral Sail
Undertow
Water Web
3rd Level
Cause Bends
Strangling Seaweed
4th Level
Desail
Farvision
Ironrope
Lunar Glare
Scalding Sea
Stonehull
5th Level
Air Sphere
Create Iceberg
Land Sail
Split Ice
8th Level
Raise Shipwreck
9th Level
Create Island
Curse of the Ancient Mariner

AIR SPHERE

Spell Level: Druid, 5th Level; Magic-User, 5th Level
Range: Centered on caster
Duration: Up to one hour

This spell creates a five-foot-wide bubble of pure, fresh air that surrounds the caster. It provides fresh, breathable air no matter the conditions outside the bubble. If underwater, the bubble also protects those inside from the drawbacks of being in a deep, underwater environment. The bubble does not prevent spells from passing through it, but those inside gain a +1 bonus to saving throws vs. noxious or poisonous gases.

The caster is lifted a few inches off the ground while inside the bubble, but cannot move the sphere. The bubble can be moved from outside, however, and sinks in water with the weight of those inside. However, when the spell is first cast, the caster can decide to move the bubble up to 20 feet in any direction. The caster can end the sphere at any time.

ANCHOR

Spell Level: Cleric, 1st Level; Magic-User, 1st Level
Range: Touch
Duration: 24 hours

The caster can touch a boat or ship and bring it to a gentle halt. Until the spell ends, the vessel can't be moved by any means. The caster can touch the vessel again to end the effect.

BALLAST

Spell Level: Druid, 2nd Level; Magic-User, 2nd Level
Range: Touch
Duration: Up to 1 hour

This spell causes an object or creature that is no larger than man-sized to be either neutrally buoyant or positively buoyant (caster's choice). If the object or creature is neutrally buoyant, it floats at its current depths. If it is a creature, it can then swim without suffering from the effects of wearing armor. If the object or creature becomes positively buoyant, it rises 30 feet at the end of each of its turns until it reaches a solid object that stops its progress or the surface of the body of water, whichever comes first.

BOARDING PLANK

Spell Level: Magic-User, 2nd Level
Range: 60 feet
Duration: Up to 10 minutes

An invisible plank of force springs into existence at a point you choose within range. The plank appears in a horizontal orientation or at an angle no greater than 45 degrees. If the plank isn't anchored on or between two solid masses (such as boats, walls, or trees), it collapses on itself, and the spell ends at the start of the caster's next turn. The plank is five feet wide and can be up to 30 feet long. It is one-quarter inch thick, and it lasts for the duration of the spell.

Nothing can physically pass through the plank. It is immune to all damage and can't be dispelled by *dispel magic*. A *disintegrate* spell destroys the plank instantly, however. The plank also extends into the Ethereal Plane, blocking ethereal travel through the plank.

BUOYANCY

Spell Level: Magic-User, 1st Level
Range: 60 feet
Duration: 5 minutes

The caster can choose up to five sinking or suffocating creatures within range. A sinking or suffocating creature ascends to the surface of the water at a rate of 10 feet per round until the spell ends. If a creature reaches the surface before the spell ends, it floats on the surface until the spell ends. An unwilling creature that succeeds on a saving throw is unaffected.

CAUSE BENDS

Spell Level: Cleric, 3rd Level; Druid, 3rd Level; Magic-User, 3rd Level
Range: 30 feet
Duration: Instantaneous

The caster targets any creature within 30 feet and causes high-pressure gas bubbles to build up in its bloodstream. This causes great pain to the target, especially if it is in water. A target on land takes 1d4 points of damage per level of the caster and its movement is halved. In water, the target takes 1d6 points of damage per level of the caster and is incapacitated. A successful saving throw means that the target takes only half damage and its movement is not affected.

CONTROL FOG

Spell Level: Cleric, 1st Level; Druid, 1st Level; Magic-User, 1st Level
Range: 120 feet
Duration: Up to 1 hour

Until the spell ends, the caster can control any freestanding fog within range inside a chosen area that is a cube up to 20 feet on a side. The area of fog controlled increases by 10 feet for each level above 1st. The caster can choose from any of the following effects and can change the effect each round to the spell's duration:

Thin. The caster causes the fog in the area to thin. If the fog's area is heavily obscured, it becomes lightly obscured. If the fog's area is lightly obscured, it no longer obscures vision. The fog remains thinned in this way until the spell ends or the caster chooses a different effect.

Thick. The caster causes the fog in the area to thicken. If the fog's area is lightly obscured, it becomes heavily obscured. If there is no fog in the area, the caster can create fog in the area. This fog spreads around corners, and its area is lightly obscured.

CREATE ICEBERG

Spell Level: Druid, 5th Level; Magic-User, 5th Level
Range: 120 feet
Duration: Instantaneous

The caster creates an iceberg up to 60 feet in diameter in an area of saltwater within range. It must be in an area with enough saltwater to support an iceberg of its size. The iceberg can have any desired shape, though it can't occupy the same space as a creature or object. If the iceberg cuts through a creature's space when it appears, the creature is pushed directly away from the center of the iceberg. The iceberg begins to melt immediately if created in a non-arctic climate

CREATE ISLAND

Spell Level: Druid, 7th Level; Magic-User, 9th Level
Range: Within sight
Duration: 30 days

The caster creates an island of bare stone up to 1 mile in diameter in an area of saltwater within range that is big enough to hold the island. The island isn't connected to the seafloor, but it remains stationary in the location where it is created. The island can have any desired shape.

Because the island's creation occurs slowly (over 10 minutes), creatures in the area can't usually be trapped or injured by the creation. Similarly, this spell doesn't directly affect plant growth in the area, and plants in the area either move with the island's creation or are pushed directly away from its center, at the Referee's discretion.

CURSE OF THE ANCIENT MARINER

Spell Level: Magic-User, 9th Level
Range: Touch
Duration: Until dispelled

The caster creates a magical curse on a touched creature. The target must succeed on a saving throw or be cursed. While cursed, the target brings bad luck onto any water-bound vessel it rides or captains. The bad luck manifests itself in a variety of ways, usually minor at first, such as minor injuries befalling crewmembers, then progressing to major, such as the wind steering the vessel into an oncoming storm, and finally ending in catastrophic events, such as a mighty sea monster attacking the vessel and sinking it. The bad luck's manifestation is at the Referee's discretion, and you are encouraged to make the curse's effects gradual and severely punishing. In all cases, the curse eventually leads to the vessel's destruction, though the cursed target always, sometimes miraculously, survives.

The curse can be ended only with a *wish* spell.

DESAIL

Spell Level: Magic-User, 4th Level
Range: 240 feet
Duration: Up to 10 minutes

The caster causes the sails of a vessel within range to shrink. If the vessel is wind-powered, its speed is halved for the duration. If the vessel is both wind and oar-powered, its speed is reduced by one-quarter instead. This spell has no effect on a vessel that doesn't have sails.

DETECT CURRENT

Spell Level: Cleric, 1st Level; Druid, 1st Level; Magic-User, 1st Level
Range: Caster
Duration: Up to 10 minutes

For the duration of the spell, the caster can sense the presence of currents within one mile. The caster knows the location of the current, the direction it is moving, and its speed.

The spell can penetrate most barriers, but it is blocked by one foot of stone, one inch of common metal, a thin sheet of lead, or three feet of wood or dirt.

DETECT FISH

Spell Level: Cleric, 1st Level; Druid, 1st Level; Magic-User, 1st Level
Range: Caster
Duration: Up to 10 minutes

For the duration of the spell, the caster can sense the presence and location of amphibious or water-breathing beasts within 60 feet. The caster can also identify the kind of beast, such as crab, shark, or tuna fish, and its general health, such as injured, suffering from an illness, or healthy.

DETECT LAND

Spell Level: Cleric, 1st Level; Druid, 1st Level; Magic-User, 1st Level
Range: Caster
Duration: Up to 10 minutes

For the duration of the spell, the caster can sense the presence of land, such as islands or a continent, within five miles. You know the direction to the land, but not its size or other features, such as terrain type. You detect only land that is above the surface of the water.

The spell can penetrate most barriers, but it is blocked by one foot of stone, one inch of common metal, a thin sheet of lead, or three feet of wood or dirt.

FARVISION

Spell Level: Cleric, 4th Level; Magic-User, 4th Level
Range: Touch
Duration: 8 hours

The caster touches a transparent object such as glass spectacles, a glass monocle, a crystal spyglass, or similar object and imbues it with magic. For the duration of the spell, a creature can place the object over at least one of its eyes and gains darkvision out to a range of 90 feet until the object is removed from its eye.

Casting this spell on the same object every day for a year makes this effect permanent.

FILL THE SAILS

Spell Level: Druid, 2nd Level; Magic-User, 2nd Level
Range: 30 feet
Duration: Up to 1 hour

This spell fills the sails of a vessel within range with swift-moving air. For the duration, the vessel's speed increases by half. For example, a vessel with a speed of 2 miles per hour moves 3 miles per hour when affected by this spell.

HARD WATER BLAST

Spell Level: Druid, 1st Level; Magic-User, 1st Level
Range: 60 feet
Duration: Instantaneous

A stream of water streaks out from the caster's palm toward a creature within range. On a hit, the target takes 1d4 points of damage and is pushed five feet away from the caster. The target can't be pushed into damaging terrain such as lava or a pit, a solid object such as a wall, or another creature.

The spell's damage increases by 1d4 for every three levels of experience. Thus, the caster is able to do 2d4 points of damage at 3rd level, 3d4 points of damage at 6th level, 4d4 points of damage at 9th level, and 5d4 at 12th level (maximum).

HARD WATER WEAPON

Spell Level: Druid, 2nd Level; Magic-User, 2nd Level
Range: Caster
Duration: 6 rounds

This spell creates a weapon of solidified water that takes the shape of any one-handed weapon usable by the caster. When the caster hits a target with the weapon, it deals normal damage for a weapon of its type plus an extra 1d6 points of cold damage. For every 5 levels of experience, the weapon deals an additional 1d6 points of damage. Thus, at 5th level, the weapon does 2d6 points of damage plus 1d6 points of cold damage. At 10th level, the weapon does 3d6 points of damage plus 1d6 points of cold damage.

IRONROPE

Spell Level: Cleric, 4th Level; Magic-User, 4th Level
Range: Touch
Duration: 24 hours

The caster touches a length of rope that is up to 100 feet long and makes it as tough as iron. The rope is immune to fire damage and a creature attempting to cut the rope must succeed on an Open Doors check with a –2 penalty to cut or snap the rope.

LAND SAIL

Spell Level: Cleric, 5th Level; Magic-User, 5th Level
Range: 60 feet
Duration: 8 hours

This spell grants a vessel within range the ability to move across any solid surface — such as dirt, ice, or rock — as if it were harmless water (vessels crossing rough terrain can still take damage from moving through the area). The vessel's movement through the solid surface leaves a narrow trench no wider or deeper than the vessel's keel in the surface as the vessel moves, with the majority of its bulk gliding above the surface.

Though this spell allows a vessel to move across a solid surface, the vessel must still have a method of propulsion. A sailing vessel needs wind to sail across a solid surface just as it does in water, and an oar-powered vessel must be poled along the ground.

If you target a beached vessel, the vessel rights itself and can be moved by its method of propulsion; however, this spell doesn't repair damage to the hull or guarantee that the vessel will be seaworthy once returned to the water. Unless supported or returned to water, the vessel grinds to a halt and falls over when the spell ends.

LUNAR GLARE

Spell Level: Druid, 4th Level; Magic-User, 4th Level
Range: 300 feet
Duration: 8 hours

The spell creates a false moon visible within five miles of the caster for the duration. The caster must be outdoors at night to cast this spell.

A shapechanger that sees the moon must succeed on a saving throw or instantly revert to its original form. It can't assume a different form until it leaves the moon's light, such as by stepping around a shadowed corner or into a building.

Tidal water within five miles of the moon rise to high tide gradually as you cast the spell. The tide remains high for the duration. Because the water's movement occurs slowly, creatures in the tidal water can't be trapped or injured by the water's movement, and objects in the water that aren't being worn or carried and plants floating in the water are carried along with the water's movement. Moored and anchored boats rise with the water's level but are otherwise unaffected by the water's movement.

RAISE SHIPWRECK

Spell Level: Magic-User, 8th Level
Range: Sight
Duration: Up to 1 hour

One sunken vessel of your choice that you can see within range rises vertically 20 feet per round until it reaches the water's surface. It floats on the surface for the duration. If the vessel is in multiple pieces, you must choose which piece to raise to the surface.

When the spell ends, the vessel sinks gently to the seafloor unless it was made seaworthy before the end of the spell.

SCALDING SEA

Spell Level: Magic-User, 4th Level
Range: 120 feet
Duration: Up to 10 minutes

The caster creates a 20-foot-radius sphere of steam on a point within range on the surface of a body of water. The steam spreads around corners, and its area is lightly obscured. It lasts for the duration or until a wind of moderate or greater speed (at least 10 miles per hour) disperses it.

The caster can superheat the steam to burn creatures in the area. Each creature in the steam takes 3d6 points of damage (or half as much with a successful saving throw). After the caster superheats the steam three times or if the duration expires, the spell ends.

SPECTRAL SAIL

Spell Level: Magic-User, 2nd Level
Range: 60 feet
Duration: 8 hours

This spell creates a spectral sail on the mast of a sailing vessel that has lost its sail or that has a sail that is tied or otherwise incapable of catching the wind to propel the vessel. The spectral sail is invisible and made of force, but it otherwise acts like a canvas sail.

SPLIT ICE

Spell Level: Druid, 5th Level; Magic-User, 5th Level
Range: 200-foot line before and behind the caster
Duration: Up to 8 hours

Sea-bound ice in a 200-foot line extending in front of and behind the caster parts in a trench that is 30 feet wide and 15 feet deep. The parted ice forms walls on either side of the caster. The trench moves with the caster and creates a passageway in front of and behind for seafaring vessels. As the caster moves away from an area that was parted, the ice slowly recombines over the course of the next round until it is restored to the way it was before this spell was cast.

The ice's splitting occurs slowly, and creatures in the area can't usually be trapped or injured by the ice's movement. Similarly, this spell doesn't directly affect plant growth. The moved ice carries any plants and creatures along with it as it splits and reforms. An unwilling creature must make a saving throw to avoid being moved with the ice, though it might find itself falling into the water of the trench created by this spell unless it is capable of flying.

This spell can target only nonmagical ice and can't harm or destroy ice created by spells or effects, such as the *wall of ice* spell.

STONEHULL

Spell Level: Druid, 4th Level; Magic-User, 4th Level
Range: 60 feet
Duration: Up to 1 hour

This spell turns the hull of a vessel within range as hard as stone. Until the spell ends, the target vessel has double the normal structural points and resists nonmagical damage.

STRANGLING SEAWEED

Spell Level: Druid, 3rd Level; Magic-User, 3rd Level
Range: 90 feet
Duration: 1 round per caster level

This spell causes squirming, green seaweed to fill a 10-foot-radius sphere on a point in the water that the caster can see within range. Any creature in the area must roll a saving throw or be restrained and takes 1d6 points of damage per round until an Open Doors check is made to escape. A boat or ship 60 feet long or shorter that enters the area of seaweed stops moving, held in place by the seaweed.

UNDERTOW

Spell Level: Druid, 2nd Level; Magic-User, 2nd Level
Range: Caster (60-foot line)
Duration: Instantaneous

While underwater, this spell causes a line of fast-moving water 60 feet long and 10 feet wide to blast from the caster in a chosen direction. Each creature caught in this rush of water is pushed 15 feet away from the caster and takes 1d4 points of damage per caster level (10d4 maximum) unless they make a saving throw for half damage. If a creature on the surface of the water fails the saving throw, it is also pulled beneath the surface of the water and begins suffocating unless it can breathe underwater.

At the Referee's discretion, the undertow can push current-driven seafaring vessels in a direction following the line.

UNSEEN PILOT

Spell Level: Magic-User, 1st Level
Range: 100 feet
Duration: 8 hours

This spell creates an invisible, mindless, shapeless force that pilots and navigates a vehicle such as a ship or wagon in the direction of your choice until the spell ends. The pilot springs into existence in an unoccupied space near a vehicle's wheel or primary controls within range. The caster can mentally command the pilot to change the direction it is steering the vehicle or stop the vehicle. The pilot drives and navigates the vehicle, but it doesn't power the vehicle.

The pilot knows basic directions and how to navigate the vehicle in most normal conditions and terrain, but it can't navigate a vehicle in uncertain or chaotic situations, such as through a storm or on a chariot chase through crowded city streets. The pilot doesn't know specific locations, nor can it read a map. It can steer the vehicle only in the direction the caster indicates.

WATER WEB

Spell Level: Magic-User, 2nd Level
Range: 60 feet
Duration: Up to 1 hour

The caster conjures a mass of tangled rope at a point underwater within range. The rope fills a 20-foot cube from that point for the duration. Any creature in the area must make a saving throw or be restrained by the tangling mass of rope. Creatures can cut their way free or make an Open Doors check to snap the restraints. If cast out of water or if raised to the surface, a five-foot cube of rope frays and fades each round.

Chapter 5: New Magic Items

Many new magical objects are described below.

Armor

Coral Armor

This unique suit of armor (AC 4[15]) is crafted out of coral. The wearer gains a swim movement of 12 while wearing it.

Wand

Wand of Air and Water Mastery

This wand has two glass orbs affixed to either end. One is filled with water and the other is filled with murky, white air. While underwater and holding the rod, the wielder gains a swim speed equal to their walking speed. While exposed to air and holding the wand, the wielder cannot be pushed or shoved by wind, such as by a strong storm or the *control winds* spell. The wielder can expend a charge from the wand to cast any of the following spells: *lower water, obscuring mist, water breathing,* or *wall of ice*.

Lesser Miscellaneous Magical Items

Brooch of the Desert

This brooch allows the wearer's equipment to remain dry even in the heaviest of storms. This brooch doesn't keep the wearer dry while immersed in water, but it dries the equipment one round after the wearer is no longer immersed.

Brooch of the Dolphin

Anyone wearing this dolphin-shaped brooch can hold their breath for up to 30 minutes per day and see clearly out to 30 feet while underwater. The sight is based on echolocation, and the wearer can't use it while deafened.

Caster's Bones

These rune-etched animal bones are rattled and dropped to activate them, at which time the wielder must choose to target himself or a creature within 60 feet. If the wielder targets himself, he gains a +1 bonus on his next attack roll. If the target is another creature, the creature must succeed on a saving throw or take a −1 penalty on its saving throw against the next spell of 3rd level or lower the wielder casts at the creature. Once used, the bones can't be used again until the next dawn.

Coral Lung

This hollow tube of coral is about one foot long with a mouthpiece at one end. While underwater, the wielder can hold the tube in the mouth and breathe air for one hour. Once emptied, the tube's reservoir of air can be refilled by holding it above water for one minute.

Compass of Pelora

While holding this compass, the wielder can target a creature within 120 feet. The compass points in the direction of the targeted creature, regardless of distance, for as long as the two are on the same plane of existence. It points to the creature's physical body whether living or dead, and it points in the direction of that target until the bearer targets a new creature.

Exile's Wood

This three-foot-long plank of wood has three pairs of leather loops, and it never sinks, no matter the weather or water conditions, as long as it doesn't support more than 1,000 pounds of weight.

Mariner's Eyepatch

This eyepatch is heavily encrusted with jewels and arcane writing. Anyone wearing this eyepatch can cast *read languages* or *detect invisibility*. Once used, the eyepatch can't be used this way again until the next dawn.

Preserved Hearts

A *preserved heart* is the magically-preserved heart from a humanoid. Different types of hearts exist, each with a different single-use effect. Each heart must be consumed to activate its power.

Courtesan. This heart once belonged to a courtesan slain by a competitor. When consumed, the wielder can cast the *charm person* spell once in the next 24 hours.

Shaman. This heart once belonged to the shaman of a nomadic tribe. When consumed, the wielder regains 3d6 hit points.

Shark Hunter. This heart once belonged to a great shark-hunting warrior who died of old age. When consumed, the wielder gains swim 12 for 24 hours. In addition, severed body parts (fingers, legs, tails, and so on), if any, are restored after two minutes. If a severed limb is held to the stump, consuming the heart also causes the limb to instantaneously knit to the stump.

Slave. This heart once belonged to an escaped slave. When consumed, movement is increased by 10 for 24 hours.

Warrior. This heart once belonged to a great warrior who died after defeating overwhelming odds. When consumed, the wielder is immune to *charm person* and *fear* spells for 24 hours.

Witch Doctor. This heart once belonged to a witch doctor whose heart was removed while the witch doctor was still breathing. When consumed, the wielder gains the ability to cast a 1st-level cleric and a 1st-level wizard spell of their choice for 24 hours.

Youth. This heart once belonged to a wrongfully-accused youth who was punished and slain for a crime. When consumed, the wielder's body grows younger, shedding 1d4+4 years of age.

Spectacles of the Sahuagin

While wearing these lenses made from carefully-preserved sahuagin eyes, the wielder gains darkvision out to a range of 60 feet and can magically command any shark within 60 feet using a limited telepathy. If the wearer already has darkvision, the spectacles increase its range by 60 feet.

Medium Miscellaneous Magical Items

Anchor of Weighing

When a command word is spoken, this ornate, pocket-sized, wooden anchor becomes a full-sized anchor. While full-sized on a boat or ship, the anchor prevents the vessel from being moved by any means for up to 24 hours. The command word can be spoken again to end this effect. Once used, the anchor doesn't function again until the next dawn.

Aquascope of the Kuah-Lij

These two lanterns are bound by a thin, silken rope that can stretch up to 500 feet. One lantern can be lowered into the water (from a dock or the side of a ship), and the wielder can speak a command word and peer into the lantern to see what the other is seeing. The lantern in the water has darkvision out to120 feet and can be rotated by turning the lantern the wielder holds.

If a lantern is dropped into a cramped space (such as into the wreckage of a ship or a coral reef), there is a 25% chance that it becomes tangled. This chance increases to 50% if the wielder is moving along the surface and pulling the underwater lantern. To untangle it, a creature must dive down and physically remove the lantern from the confines.

Bamboo Skiff

This small skiff is made from linked bamboo poles. It is 10 feet long, four feet wide, and two feet deep, and can hold up to four passengers. A wielder can speak a command word while grasping the tiller to cause the skiff to move up to 60 feet in a chosen direction. While within three miles of a coast or reef, the skiff can't be capsized, no matter how violent the weather or movement of its occupants.

Boots of the Waves

While wearing these calf-high boots, the wearer gains a +1 bonus to saving throws against being pushed, pulled, or knocked prone by strong winds and waves or the movement of a ship at sea. In addition, the wearer gains the same +1 bonus against spells or features that push, pull, or knock prone by creating or manipulating wind or water, such as the spell *control winds,* or the attacks of air or water elementals.

Bottled Cloud

This clear crystal bottle swirls with white, fluffy clouds and weighs one pound. When the stopper is removed, a cloud up to 40 feet long, up to 10 feet wide, and one foot thick appears. It flows along the ground out of the bottle to form a solid, but fluffy, surface after one round. It stays together even over openings in the ground, allowing it to form a bridge across a pit or chasm as long as at least five feet of the cloud is on a solid surface. Once formed, the cloud is immobile and can support up to 500 pounds. A command word returns the cloud to the bottle or it disperses on its own after one hour. Strong winds can disperse it in one minute. One used, the cloud can't be summoned again until dawn of the next cloudy day.

Derelict's Chartbook

This large chartbook contains maps, charts, and notes penned ages ago by sailors since lost to time. It is waterproof, suffering no ill effects from being submerged or stored in a humid location. If a page is damaged, destroyed, or removed, it is magically repaired by the next dawn. The book can be used to cast *control weather* once every seven days.

Hospitality's Hammock

This hammock is spun of the finest spider silk. When someone rests overnight in this hammock, they recover from either a disease, blindness, deafness, paralysis, or poison.

Sextant of Seeming

While holding this sextant inside a seafaring vessel, the wielder can cast a powerful *phantasmal force* on the vessel. The illusion lasts for up to 24 hours or until dismissed or dispelled. Once used, the spell can't be cast again until the next dawn.

Greater Miscellaneous Magical Items

Ballasts of Buoyancy

These barrels come in a set of four. While all four barrels are affixed to a larger ship (a ship requiring a crew of 20 or more to function), a command word can be spoken to raise the ship out of the water to reduce the vessel's draft (the vertical distance from the waterline to the bottom of the hull) by 50%. This can allow larger ships to traverse shallower waterways.

Captain's Horn

These small, gold hoop earrings come in a set of 10: one captain's pair and four officer pairs. Anyone wearing one pair of the earrings can communicate telepathically with any creature within 60 feet that is also wearing one of the pairs of earrings in this set. Anyone wearing the captain's pair of earrings can send a single, telepathic message to all creatures within 60 feet that are wearing pairs of the officer earrings.

If the captain's pair of earrings is destroyed, all of the pairs of earrings become nonmagical.

Deep Suit of the Kuah-Lij

This wetsuit is light, flexible, and comes with an attached cowl. It can be worn under normal clothes. While wearing this wetsuit with its cowl up, the wearer can breathe underwater and gains a swimming speed equal to their walking speed. In addition, the wearer is immune to cold damage while immersed in water and cannot be affected by a deep, underwater environment.

Some variations of the wetsuit come with a *light* spell enchanted on the top of the cowl, which can be activated by speaking its command word.

Lung Leaf

This large leaf is a deep, rich blue and has silver veins running through it. Anyone consuming the leaf can breathe underwater for eight hours and gains a swim speed equal to their walking speed.

Sahuagin's Dismay

This tattered, green flag bears the image of a red trident. While this flag flies on the mast of a ship, the ship and its crew are protected from nonmagical extreme weather. The temperature on the ship is always cool, windspeeds never go higher than strong, and precipitation that falls on the ship is never heavier than a steady mist. The flag also protects the ship from begin swamped by even the largest waves, though strong currents still affect the ship. The flag doesn't protect the ship from predation by sea creatures or from being capsized or sunk by such creatures.

Unique Magical Items

Dissension's Digit

Castagil was a great captain of the piratical sort. Aboard the mighty galleon *The Sea Wench*, he and his crew plundered the seas for nearly a decade. Castagil was a nautical genius and a practicing mage. His skills of captaining and his command of water were outshone only by his lust for gold.

Night had fallen on the 45th day of an unrelenting search for the gold of Captain Moritire Nightshade, famed pirate captain ages gone. The crew was weary, the provision barrels were empty, and the ship wasn't a league closer to the famed treasure. That night as a storm brewed in the north, mutiny brewed in the barracks. The crew took Castagil in his sleep, beat him, and bound him in the cargo hold.

The next day, the ship set anchor near a small uncharted island. The quartermaster and six others dragged Castagil to shore, intending to maroon him with nothing more than a dirk. In the distance they heard a rumbling, and ash flitted through the air. They marched Castagil no more than a hundred yards into the jungle and came upon a trembling volcano. With their cutlasses they prodded their former captain up to the rim and pushed him in. As he plummeted toward the lava, he summoned all his magic into one curse. When he hit the lava, the volcano erupted so violently that boulders the size of wagons crashed into the hull of the ship, sinking it. As the dust and ash settled, it was revealed that the entire island had been razed. The only thing that remained was a small, glowing sphere.

Dissension's digit is a red crystal globe about two inches in diameter. When used, it glows with the oozing, red light of lava. *Dissension's digit* has the following properties:

- +1 bonus to saving throws
- Bearer is immune to fire
- Vulnerable to cold (double damage)
- The globe has five charges and regains 1d4 + 1 expended charges daily at dawn. The bearer can expend one or more charges to cast the following spells: *fire storm* (2 charges), *locate object* (must be an object made of gold or other precious substance, 1 charge), *protection from lightning* (1 charge), or *teleport* (3 charges).

Castagil's greed curses this item. Each time the bearer is within 30 feet of an object worth 100 gp or more, they must succeed on a saving throw or do everything in their power to hold and possess the object. The bearer is unwilling to part with objects worth 100 gp or more unless it leads to possessing an even more valuable item. The bearer is also unwilling to part with *dissension's digit* unless a *remove curse* spell is cast.

Dissension's digit can be destroyed only by a good-aligned spellcaster casting *remove curse* on the item twice and then throwing it into an active volcano.

Moonsilver Orb

When the coralites, first arrived at their current home, they found a quiet coral reef that was pounded by surf and often wracked by tropical storms. For many centuries, the coralites huddled together in island caves as they watched their homes sweep away with the wind.

With the advent of the magical songchangers, the creations of the coralites became more sophisticated and increasingly infused with magic. The *Moonsilver Orb* was conceived to bring the same peace to nature that the coralites had achieved in society. Calm winds and placid seas were the result.

The *Moonsilver Orb* is composed of sand from the ocean floor, silver from the Elemental Plane of Earth, and moonlight gathered on a moonless night. The orb is a silver, glass sphere about four inches in diameter with mist swirling inside it.

The *Moonsilver Orb* has the following properties:

- The bearer of the orb can speak aquan, breathe underwater, gains swim 12, and ignores the drawbacks caused by a deep, underwater environment (cold and pressure).
- The weather within one mile of the bearer is warm with light clouds and a moderate wind, no matter the weather conditions outside of that mile.
- The orb has 7 charges and regains 1d4 + 3 expended charges daily at dawn. The caster can use one or more charges to cast the following spells: *animal summoning I* (water-based animals only, 1 charges), *control winds* (2 charges), *control weather* (2 charges), or *conjure elemental* (water only, 3 charges).
- The wielder can create a whirlpool on a point of water within one mile that lasts for up to 10 minutes. Each creature within 100 feet of the whirlpool must succeed on a saving throw or be pulled 30 feet closer to the center of the whirlpool. A creature that starts its turn in the center of the whirlpool must succeed on a saving throw with a −3 penalty or be pulled underwater and begin suffocating if it can't breathe underwater. A creature pulled underwater in the center of the whirlpool takes 6d6 points of damage on a failed save, or half as much damage on a successful one. The *Moonsilver Orb* can't be used in this way again until seven days pass.

Cursed Items

Shudderer's Cowl

Anyone wearing this cloak in bright or dim light automatically takes half damage from cold (or one-quarter damage with a successful saving throw). However, the cowl is cursed, so that once donned, it cannot be removed unless a *remove curse* is cast. Also, in darkness, the wearer is vulnerable to cold, suffering a −1 penalty to saving throws and taking double damage.

Wheel of Chaos

This ornately-decorated ship's wheel is inlaid with symbols of chaos and destruction. While the wheel is affixed to a ship big enough for a crew of at least 10, the ship's speed is increased by 25%. In addition, the wielder can cast the *control weather* spell with it. The wheel can't be used this way again until five days have passed.

However, this wheel is cursed and affixing it to a ship extends the curse to the ship. Once affixed to a ship, the wheel can't be removed unless the ship is targeted by the *remove curse* spell or similar magic. While the wheel is affixed to a ship, denizens of the sea are attracted to the ship, from normal fish and sharks to larger monstrosities drawn up from the depths.

CHAPTER 6: NEW MONSTERS

New creatures are presented here to enrich any campaign based on the sea.

BLUE-FINNED VANT

Hit Dice: 4
Armor Class: 4[15]
Attacks: bite (1d6)
Saving Throw: 13
Special: pressure shift, resist cold
Move: 12 (swimming)
Alignment: Neutrality
Number Encountered: 1, 1d8+4, 3d8
Challenge Level: 5/240

Blue-finned vants are about four feet long, with broad, thick-ribbed fins across their backs. They are glittery blue in color, with a white underbelly. The tropical fish can control the water pressure around them. They dwell in or near deep coral reefs, particularly near the edges of undersea trenches. They usually go their way alone or in small schools, nibbling on coral encrustations with their bony, beak-like mouths, but can sometimes be found hunting in deeper waters. Blue-finned vants rely upon their ability to control the water pressure around them to drive off or harm potential predators, or to allow them to flee to depths that would crush most other creatures. Three times per day, a blue-finned vant can suddenly discharge water around it. Every creature within 10 feet takes 2d6 points of damage and is pushed 10 feet away from the vant. On a successful save, the creature takes half damage and is not pushed away.

Blue-Finned Vant: HD 4; AC 4[15]; Atk bite (1d6); **Move** 12; **Save** 13; **AL** N; **CL/XP** 5/240; **Special:** pressure shift (3/day, 2d6 damage and pushed 10 feet away, save for half and resist being moved), resist cold (50%).

BONJO TOMBO

Hit Dice: 14 (100 HP)
Armor Class: 0[19]
Attacks: 2 claws (2d8)
Saving Throw: 3
Special: darkvision, deafening roar, fling, immune to electricity and poison, rend, resist cold and fire (50%).
Move: 18/24 (climbing)
Alignment: Chaos
Number Encountered: 1
Challenge Level: 18/3800

Bonjo Tombo is a gorilla-like creature of truly monstrous proportions. It is a hulking brute nearly 50 feet tall at the shoulder with two pairs of yellowish eyes on either side of its horrific face, one atop the other. The beast has a wide simian mouth exposing a pair of huge curving tusks that protrude from its powerful lower jaw. Nearly hairless, its massive frame ripples with muscle beneath its filthy grayish skin. It has long arms that end in huge clawed hands and short powerful legs that end in apish feet.

Bonjo Tombo, the huge Demon Ape, is dumb, fierce, and thoroughly evil. Spawn of a two-headed demon prince and a fiendish dire ape, Bonjo Tombo rules his jungle island through malice, fear, and primeval cruelty. Although enormous, Bonjo Tombo is adept at hiding in the thick jungle vegetation of his island, his shaggy gray fur blending into the surrounding terrain.

Bonjo Tombo dislikes running water and refuses to cross it. This may be counted as a blessing by many, as it has kept him upon his island and away from the more civilized locales of the world.

At the onset of any fight, Bonjo Tombo attempts to shatter the will of his foes with an ear-splitting roar.

Bonjo Tombo: HD 14; HP 100; AC 0[19]; Atk 2 claws (2d8), bite (3d6); **Move** 18 (climb 24); **Save** 3; **AL** C; **CL/XP** 18/3800; **Special:** darkvision (60ft), deafening roar (3/day, 100ft radius, save or deafened 2d6 rounds), fling (if 2 claws hit, fling victim up to 100ft, 10d6 points of damage), immune (electricity and poison), rend (2 claws hit, rend for automatic 2d8 points of damage), resist cold and fire (50%).

BREATH TAKER

Hit Dice: 6
Armor Class: 5[14]
Attacks: 2 claws (1d6 + steal breath)
Saving Throw: 11
Special: breath eater, steal breath
Move: 9/12 (swimming)
Alignment: Chaos
Number Encountered: 1, 1d6+2
Challenge Level: 8/800

Anyone hit by one of the breath taker's claws must make a saving throw or begin to suffocate. The target continues to suffocate while within 30 feet of the breath taker. If a humanoid dies from suffocation or exhaustion while within 30 feet of the breath taker, it rises 24 hours later as a breath taker.

For every suffocating creature within 30 feet of the breath taker, the breath taker's armor class increases by 1 and it gains a +1 to-hit bonus. For example, if three suffocating swimmers are within 30 feet of the creature, the breath taker's armor class is 2[17] and it has a +3 to-hit bonus.

Breath Taker: HD 6; AC 5[14]; Atk 2 claws (1d6 + steal breath); **Move** 9 (swim 12); **Save** 11; **AL** C; **CL/XP** 8/800; **Special:** breath eater (if a suffocating creature is within 30ft, breath taker gains cumulative +1 AC bonus and −1 to-hit bonus), steal breath (if claw hits, save or begin to suffocate, suffocation continues while within 30ft of breath taker).

CORALITE

Hit Dice: 3
Armor Class: 7[12]
Attacks: spear (1d6)
Saving Throw: 14
Special: sudden inspiration
Move: 12/12 (swimming)
Alignment: Lawful
Number Encountered: 1, 1d4, 2d6
Challenge Level: 3/60

Coralites are humanoids standing four to five feet tall with a bulky build. Their skin is a deep, rich brown, and their hair is long, dark, and streaked with red or blonde. Both men and women wear garments of diaphanous silk in bright, vibrant colors to reflect a living coral reef.

Coralite culture and society are founded on one overriding principle: peace. They strongly oppose combat and violence of all types and attempt to live in peaceful relations with all of their neighbors. Overcoming their abhorrence of violence is a significant challenge to their effectiveness at combat.

From birth, coralite children are taught history, religion, spellcraft, and the arts: music, poetry, painting, sculpting, and literature. The coralites are universally skilled at some artistic endeavor, and they follow it their whole life. They are also quite skilled at performing, and even those who don't study music can recite poetry. This upbringing allows them to analyze any situation and receive a burst of sudden inspiration three times per day. They can roll 1d4 and add the results to any to-hit roll, damage, or saving throw.

Coralite: HD 3; **AC** 7[12]; **Atk** spear (1d6); **Move** 12 (swim 12); **Save** 14; **AL** L; **CL/XP** 3/60; **Special:** sudden inspiration (3/day, roll 1d4 and add result to roll to hit, damage, or saves).
Equipment: spear.

CORALITE SONGCHANGERS

The songchangers are the offspring of the coralites' marriage of magic and music. Songchanger wizards have learned to manipulate the very elemental matter of creation through song and music. They weave powerful magic into their musical compositions and are revered even above the priests in coralite society.

Coralite Songchanger: HD 7; **AC** 7[12] or 2[17] (missile) and 4[15] (melee) from *shield* spell; **Atk** staff (1d6) or dagger (1d4); **Move** 12 (swim 12); **Save** 9; **AL** L; **CL/XP** 8/800; **Special:** spells (4/3/2/1), sudden inspiration (3/day, roll 1d4 and add result to roll to hit, damage, or saves).
Spells: 1st—*charm person, light, shield, sleep*; 2nd—*invisibility, mirror image, phantasmal force*; 3rd—*hold person, suggestion*; 4th—*confusion*.
Equipment: staff or dagger.

DECK DEVIL

Hit Dice: 8
Armor Class: 4[15]
Attacks: bite (1d6 + grab), tail (2d6)
Saving Throw: 8
Special: grab, trampling glide, water leap
Move: 3/12 (swimming)
Alignment: Chaos
Number Encountered: 1, 1d4+2
Challenge Level: 8/800

Deck devils are large porpoise-like creatures with greatly elongated flippers and razor-sharp teeth.

These voracious sea creatures resemble porpoises at first glance, but they are quite unlike their docile cousins. Deck devils have a reputation as being bloodthirsty maneaters. They are carnivorous and use their innocent appearance to move in close to oncoming ships, at which point they attack any sailors they see. These aquatic creatures travel in small schools and are quite territorial. Battles between rival pods stir up the ocean to a froth of sea foam and spilled blood.

The deck devil can fly up to 30 feet each round, but it must start its movement in water. If it is flying at the end of its turn, it falls and takes falling damage.

If the deck devil is flying and moves at least 20 feet straight toward a creature then hits it with a tail attack on the same turn, that target must succeed on a saving throw or be knocked prone. The deck devil can make one bite attack against a prone creature as it swoops by.

Deck Devil: HD 8; **AC** 4[15]; **Atk** bite (1d6 + grab), tail (2d6); **Move** 3 (swim 12); **Save** 8; **AL** C; **CL/XP** 8/800; **Special:** grab (after successful bite, save or creature locks jaws on target for automatic 1d6 damage per round), trampling glide (if flying at least 20 feet and hits target with tail attack, target must save or be knocked prone and deck devil can

make additional bite attack), water leap (30ft flight out of water).

ELF, SEA

Hit Dice: 2
Armor Class: 7[12]
Attacks: weapon (1d6)
Saving Throw: 16
Special: amphibious
Move: 9/12 (swimming)
Alignment: Neutrality or Lawful
Number Encountered: 1, 1d4+1, 2d8+4
Challenge Level: 2/30

Similar to their land-bound cousins, sea elves are slender and long-lived. Their skin varies in shades of blue and purple, and their hair often resembles seaweed. Sea elves fight to defend themselves and their homes but are, on the whole, a peaceful race. Should the need to fight arise, a sea elf uses whatever means is at its disposal. They spend their years separate from the surface races, studying the many ancient ruins and shipwrecks that dot their realm. They often fight with tridents and some are accomplished spellcasters.

Sea Elf: HD 2; **AC** 7[12]; **Atk** weapon (1d6); **Move** 9 (swim 12); **Save** 16; **AL** N or L; **CL/XP** 2/30; **Special:** amphibious (can breathe on land as well as in water).

GLASS WHALE

Hit Dice: 16 (80 hit points)
Armor Class: 3[16]
Attacks: bite (3d8 + swallow whole), tail slap (4d8)
Saving Throw: 3
Special: +1 or better magic weapons to hit, illumination, passenger compartment, shatter
Move: 24 (swimming)
Alignment: Neutrality
Number Encountered: 1
Challenge Level: 18/3800

A glass whale is a whale-shaped construct composed entirely of thick, clear glass that researchers can use to travel the depths of the ocean. The body is fashioned with a dorsal hump, medium-sized flippers, and a powerful fluke that is as sharp and deadly as broken glass. Its huge, bulky head takes up nearly a third of its total body length. A single, angled blowhole is located on the far left top of its forehead, and the slim and narrow lower jaw of the glass whale is lined with peg-like teeth that fit into grooves along its robust upper jaw.

The glass whale is not primarily designed for combat. Though imparted with modest offensive ability to protect itself and its passengers, the primary function of its powerful jaw is to collect deep ocean specimens. It grabs and swallows creatures into a throat compartment it can fill with water.

If there is no water in the throat compartment, the door between the throat compartment and the interior chamber can be opened to allow a swallowed creature access to the interior chamber. The glass whale is capable of holding up to four creatures in this interior compartment. The whale's controller rides within this chamber and can issue simple commands. The compartment holds 24 hours of air. To replenish the air supply, the glass whale must breach the water's surface and collect air through its blowhole for five minutes.

The whale bites opponents with its massive mouth. If the to-hit roll is 15 or greater, the target must make a saving throw or be swallowed whole and held in the empty throat cavity where it drowns if water is allowed to fill the void. The whale can also slap with its tail.

If a glass whale is killed, it explodes in a concussive blast that sends shards of glass out to strike anyone within 10 feet of the construct.

Glass Whale: HD 16 (80 hit points); **AC** 3[16]; **Atk** bite (3d8 + swallow whole), tail slap (4d8); **Move** 24 (swim); **Save** 3; **AL** N; **CL/XP** 18/3800; **Special:** +1 or better magic weapons to hit, illumination (sheds bright light in 20ft radius), passenger compartment (hollow body can hold up to 4 creatures with air for 24 hours), shatter (upon death, explodes into glass shards, anyone within 10ft takes 4d10 damage, save for half; creatures inside save with –1 penalty).

GLOWFLUME SWARM

Hit Dice: 7
Armor Class: 5[14]
Attacks: consume flesh (3d6)
Saving Throw: 9
Special: hypnotic illumination
Move: 12 (swimming)
Alignment: Neutrality
Number Encountered: 1, 1d3+1
Challenge Level: 9/1100

A glowflume swarm is a group of tiny, carnivorous plants that gathers on the sea's surface and produces a brilliant display of colors to attract prey.

The glowflume's hypnotic glow draws in fish and sea travelers alike, charming them with the light display unless they succeed on a saving throw. Creatures drawn by the glow swim into the swarm of glowflume only to discover too late the danger they face as the tiny, flesh-eating plants devour the captivated creature.

Glowflume most commonly grows near reefs and other shallow seas where it can easily draw in land-bound creatures. The glowflume primarily consumes flesh, often leaving organs and bones in its wake.

Glowflume Swarm: HD 7; **AC** 5[14]; **Atk** consume flesh (3d6); **Move** 12 (swim); **Save** 9; **AL** N; **CL/XP** 9/1100; **Special:** hypnotic illumination (anyone within 30ft save or travel directly into swarm, as *charm person*).

HYDROPHANT

Hit Dice: 8
Armor Class: 5[14]
Attacks: 2 slams (1d6 + engulf), tail slap (1d8)
Saving Throw: 8
Special: +1 or better magic weapons to hit, engulf, false appearance, stunning slam
Move: 6/18 (swimming)
Alignment: Chaos
Number Encountered: 1, 1d4
Challenge Level: 9/1100

The hydrophant is a hulking, legless humanoid composed entirely of thousands of moist, diaphanous bubbles. The lower torso develops into a large fluke similar to a whale's. Two oval-shaped, dark blue water cavities serve as its eyes, while a dense cluster of gray-colored bubbles line the recess that marks its mouth.

The hydrophant is a cantankerous elemental culmination of air and water, renowned for its cruel and territorial nature.

The hydrophant strikes with two slams and a tail slap. If it hits with both slams, the target must make a saving throw or be drawn into the creature and held. While trapped, the creature takes 1d8 points of damage each round. It must make an Open Doors check to escape.

Three times per day wcan slam andrupturetakes 2d6 points of damage and is stunned for 1d4 rounds. successful saving throw While motionless, the hydrophant appears to be a large patch of bubbles and has a 1-in-6 chance of going unnoticed.

Hydrophant: HD 8; **AC** 5[14]; **Atk** 2 slams (1d6 + engulf), tail slap (1d8); **Move** 6 (swim 18); **Save** 8; **AL** C; **CL/XP** 9/1100; **Special:** +1 or better magic weapons to hit, engulf (if both slams hit target, save or held for automatic 1d8 damage, Open Doors check to escape), false appearance (while motionless, 1-in-6 chance to notice), stunning slam (3/day, 2d6 damage and stunned for 1d4 rounds, save for half).

KEEL KELP

Hit Dice: 8
Armor Class: 6[13]
Attacks: 4 kelp strands (1d6 + squeeze)
Saving Throw: 8
Special: false appearance, immune to cold, resist fire, squeeze
Move: 3/24 (swimming)
Alignment: Neutrality
Number Encountered: 1
Challenge Level: 8/800

Keel kelp is semi-sentient plant that lives within two to four miles of certain tropical islands. From the bow of a ship, keel kelp appears to be nothing more than a large floating mass of tangled seaweed and kelp. If found near coral or rocky areas, it is likely to be interwoven with kelp of the standard variety.

Keel kelp hardens and sticks to ships that pass over it, entangling and slowing the ship. The keel kelp is equally happy slowly digesting the wood of the ship or the creatures inside. Against particularly sturdy ships, the keel kelp lashes out at the creatures on board, seeking easier prey. While motionless, keel kelp appears to be harmless kelp.

Keel Kelp: HD 8; **AC** 6[13]; **Atk** 4 kelp strands (1d6 + squeeze); **Move** 3 (swim 24); **Save** 8; **AL** N; **CL/XP** 8/800; **Special:** false appearance (appears to be kelp), immune to cold, resist fire (50%), squeeze (save or automatic 1d6 damage, 25% chance of random limb pinned).

KULGREER

Hit Dice: 9
Armor Class: 6[13]
Attacks: 2 slams (1d8), bite (2d6 + grab)
Saving Throw: 6
Special: +1 or better magic weapons to hit, grab, immune to cold, swallow whole, whirlpool
Move: 18 (swimming)
Alignment: Chaos
Number Encountered: 1, 1d4+2
Challenge Level: 12/2000

A kulgreer is a massive, abominable being of the deep sea that creates powerful whirlpools inside its funnel-like body. It has a 30-foot-long conical body resembling a funnel, beginning in a wide mouth 30 feet in diameter and tapering into a five-foot-diameter outlet of dim, white light.

The kulgreer navigates the depths in a non-cognizant state, pointed-end first; its conical body gradually rotates and propels itself forward subconsciously, amassing various creatures into its frame as it passes through. If awakened from this state, the kulgreer is generally violent.

It is popular belief that creatures sucked into the kulgreer's funnel-like body are teleported to another plane of existence. Three times per day, a kulgreer can generate a whirlpool around itself that bludgeons creatures as it draws them to the creature.

Kulgreer: HD 9; **AC** 6[13]; **Atk** 2 slams (1d8), bite (2d6 + grab); **Move** 18 (swim); **Save** 6; **AL** C; **CL/XP** 12/2000;

Special: +1 or better magic weapons to hit, grab (after bite, save or held and automatic 2d6 damage per round), immune to cold, swallow whole (natural 20 to hit, automatic 2d6 damage), whirlpool (3/day, any creature within 30ft must save or be drawn into current and bludgeoned for 8d6 damage).

LAMPREY, BURROWING

Hit Dice: 3
Armor Class: 6[13]
Attacks: bite (1d6 + blood drain)
Saving Throw: 14
Special: blood drain, burrow
Move: 6/12 (swimming)
Alignment: Neutrality
Number Encountered: 1, 1d4+2, 2d6
Challenge Level: 4/120

The burrowing lamprey is an eel-like fish that attaches to its prey, then burrows into its body, feasting on blood and the rich vital organs.

If the lamprey bites a creature, the target must make a saving throw or the lamprey attaches. The target takes 1d4 points of damage each round from blood loss. If the lamprey makes a bite attack while attached, it burrows into the flesh of the target and curls up inside to feed. The target takes 2d4 points of damage each round from the poisonous intruder. The lamprey can be cut out, but doing so requires dealing 2d8 points of damage to the host.

Burrowing Lamprey: HD 3; AC 6[13]; Atk bite (1d6 + blood drain); Move 6 (swim 12); Save 14; AL N; CL/XP 4/120; Special: blood drain (after bite, save or lamprey attaches and drains 1d4 blood per round), burrow (if attached to drain blood, successful bite attack lets lamprey burrow inside creature, host takes 2d4 damage each round, can be cut out by doing 2d8 damage to host).

NISP

Nisps resemble hairless humanoids with smooth, slick skin; their hands and feet are webbed and end in claws, and their faces have large, dark pupil-less eyes. They have no noses or ears, and their small fishlike mouths are filled with tiny, sharp teeth. They are a
race of water-based fey creatures that dwell in swamps, rivers, lakes, and seas.

BURGUNDY NISP

Hit Dice: 4
Armor Class: 4[15]
Attacks: 2 claws (1d6), bite (1d8)
Saving Throw: 13
Special: rend, surprise
Move: 6/18 (swimming)
Alignment: Neutrality
Number Encountered: 1, 1d6, 2d8
Challenge Level: 4/120

Burgundy nisps have dark, burgundy skin with bellies that lighten to a pale vermilion. They often lurk near the surface, especially under boats or piers, and launch themselves from the water to attack their prey. They live in underwater caves and hollows, often in families and small clans. They may pick up and move to another area frequently or stay in a place for years. They avoid other underwater races and almost certainly avoid living near a community of such beings.

Burgandy Nisp: HD 4; AC 4[15]; Atk 2 claws (1d6), bite (1d8); **Move** 6 (swim 18); **Save** 13; **AL** N; **CL/XP** 4/120; **Special:** rend (if 2 claws hit, additional 2d6 damage), surprise (1–3 on 1d6).

CRESTED NISP

Hit Dice: 6
Armor Class: 4[15]
Attacks: 2 claws (1d6), bite (1d8)
Saving Throw: 11
Special: rend, spell-like abilities
Move: 6/18 (swimming)
Alignment: Neutrality
Number Encountered: 1, 1d6, 2d8
Challenge Level: 6/400

Crested nisps have sleek, colored hides with a finned crest running along their heads and down their spine. These crested nisps are solitary, territorial creatures that prefer to dwell in coral reefs or rocky shoals, often in coastal waters. Because of their affinity with creatures of the sea, they often have predatory marine life positioned strategically about their lairs and are often accompanied by sharks, large eels, or other defenders. They maintain one area for their entire lives, never seeking to leave it, and they become riled when their territory is invaded. When a crested nisp is seriously injured, it retreats to its lair, trusting carefully-placed sea creatures and hazards to weaken or drive off pursuers while it regains its strength.

Crested Nisp: HD 6; AC 4[15]; Atk 2 claws (1d6), bite (1d8); **Move** 6 (swim 18); **Save** 11; **AL** C; **CL/XP** 6/400; **Special:** rend (if 2 claws hit, additional 2d6 damage), spell-like abilities.
Spell-like abilities: at will—*speak with animals*; 3/day—*faerie fire, locate animals*; 1/day—*animal summoning I*.

SPANGLED NISP

Hit Dice: 3
Armor Class: 4[15]
Attacks: 2 claws (1d6), bite (1d8)
Saving Throw: 14
Special: fearful
Move: 6/18 (swimming)
Alignment: Neutrality
Number Encountered: 1, 1d6, 2d8
Challenge Level: 3/60

Spangled nisps are the weakest of the species and named for their pallid skin speckled with moles of various colors. They are the most cowardly and inoffensive of the species, fleeing whenever confronted. However, they do feel the curiosity innate in their species and often come to shore in the dark to rummage through the refuse of land-dweller settlements. Some primitive cultures allow spangled nisps to co-exist, often feeding the nisps in exchange for warnings when outsiders approach. The nisps can understand a few basic words of nearby communities' languages, but they don't speak. Because of their innate cowardice, the spangled nisp flees from any confrontation with a creature its size or larger and may even back down from smaller creatures if the creatures put on a bold enough display. If cornered, spangled nisps defend themselves and seek to escape as soon as possible.

Spangled Nisp: HD 3; AC 4[15]; Atk 2 claws (1d6), bite (1d8); **Move** 6 (swim 18); **Save** 14; **AL** N; **CL/XP** 3/60; **Special:** fearful (50% chance to flee conflicts).

Sail Moth Swarm

Hit Dice: 8
Armor Class: 6[13]
Attacks: bite (3d6)
Saving Throw: 8
Special: salt sense
Move: 3/12 (flying)
Alignment: Neutrality
Number Encountered: 1
Challenge Level: 8/800

Sail moths are much like standard moths, save they are somewhat more aggressive and sustain themselves on salt, which they seek out. Unable to feast on salt directly from the water, they look for more available salt deposits, namely the fabric found aboard ships that travel the salty oceans. Few sights are more feared by veteran mariners than a gray cloud of sail moths moving toward the ship's vulnerable sails, for in a matter of minutes, the moths can reduce a sail to tatters.

Sail Moth Swarm: HD 8; AC 6[13]; Atk bite (3d6); **Move** 3 (fly 12); **Save** 8; **AL** N; **CL/XP** 8/800; **Special:** salt sense (locate salt [meat, sails, sweat, etc.] within 120 ft).

Sea Serpents

Nearly as old as the dragons that roam the sky are the sea serpents, great snakelike creatures that have roamed the oceans for ages. Unlike the classical dragon, these great, scaly, serpentine beasts are generally agreed to be a product of evolution, though many suspect magical influence, either deliberate or natural, somewhere in their evolution.

Whatever their origins, sea serpents are a highly varied species, with a great variation in size, coloration, intellect, and temperament. However, all sea serpents bear certain similarities. They are long, serpentine, warm- blooded creatures that closely resemble snakes in appearance, though they all have two sets of flippers, which may be large or so small and atrophied as to be nearly unnoticeable. Sea serpents are aquatic creatures, though some can make their way about on land. All sea serpents can breathe both water and air with equal efficiency, and they all possess some level of sentience. Sea serpent bites are venomous, and their sinuous bodies are built for constricting and crushing prey. The largest sea serpents often wrap themselves around seagoing vessels, devouring the sailors on board. Like their draconic cousins, sea serpents have a sense of innate superiority, feeling they are masters of the sea. They aren't beyond reason and can often be bribed or intimidated into leaving a vessel and its occupants alone.

Arctic Sea Serpent

Hit Dice: 12
Armor Class: 4[15]
Attacks: bite (1d8 + constrict)
Saving Throw: 3
Special: constrict, immune to cold and poison, spell-like abilities, vulnerable to fire
Move: 6/18 (swimming)
Alignment: Chaos
Number Encountered: 1, 1d2
Challenge Level: 13/2300

Arctic Sea Serpent: HD 12; AC 4[15]; Atk bite (1d8 + constrict); **Move** 6 (swim 18); **Save** 3; **AL** C; **CL/XP** 13/2300; **Special:** constrict (save or held, automatic 2d6 damage), immune to cold and poison, spell-like abilities, vulnerable to

fire (200%).
Spell-like abilities: at will—*detect magic, magic missile, phantasmal force*; 3/day—*dispel magic, invisibility*; 1/day—*fly, haste*.

Fluting Sea Serpent

Hit Dice: 10
Armor Class: 3[16]
Attacks: bite (1d8 + poison + constrict)
Saving Throw: 5
Special: constrict, fluting song, poison, spell-like abilities
Move: 18 (swimming)
Alignment: Chaos
Number Encountered: 1, 1d3
Challenge Level: 13/2300

This serpent's body scales are smooth and deep green in color with a blue-gray undertone. It has wide flippers that enable it to move about slowly on land. It speaks with a musical voice reminiscent of the sound of a flute. The fluting sea serpent is an intelligent serpent known for its masterful singing. Though highly individualistic, they may sometimes be hired by civilized beings to serve as court bards, particularly for undersea races. Fluting sea serpents usually live in sea caves along ocean shores, and they love performing and learning. Creatures often seek them out for information on a particular esoteric subject or to listen to a particular performance. Battle is a last resort for the fluting sea serpent, which prefers negotiation. However, fluting sea serpents can be unpredictable, particularly when their performances are faulted, which may cause them to fly into a sulky rage. Anyone who hears their fluting roar must save or flee in fear.

Fluting Sea Serpent: HD 10; AC 3[16]; Atk bite (1d8 + poison + constrict); **Move** 18 (swimming); **Save** 5; **AL** C; **CL/XP** 13/2300; **Special:** constrict (save or held, automatic 2d6 damage), fluting song (30ft range, save or flee in fear as spell), poison (save or additional 1d6 damage), spell-like abilities.
Spell-like abilities: at will—*detect magic*; 3/day—*charm person, phantasmal force*; 1/day—*hold person, suggestion*.

Undead Sea Serpent

Hit Dice: 13
Armor Class: 0[19]
Attacks: 1d8 (1d8 + poison + constrict)
Saving Throw: 3
Special: constrict, immune to sleep and charm, magic resistance, poison
Move: 18 (swimming)
Alignment: Chaos
Number Encountered: 1
Challenge Level: 16/3200

By some quirk of their biology, sea serpents slain by magic have a high chance of becoming one of the restless dead. This quirk leads many scholars to theorize the original sea serpents were not naturally-occurring creatures and were instead magical creations made by some great sea-faring arcanist millennia ago. Undead sea serpents share several traits in common, no matter the type of sea serpents they were in life. Undead sea serpents are immune to *sleep* and *charm* spells and are resistant to magic (25%). The poison injected by the bite of an undead sea serpent forces a target to make a saving throw or be paralyzed for 1d4+1 rounds.

Undead Sea Serpent: HD 13; AC 0[19]; Atk bite (1d8 + poison + constrict); **Move** 18 (swim); **Save** 3; **AL** C; **CL/**

XP 16/3200; **Special:** constrict (save or held, automatic 2d6 damage), immune to charm and fear, magic resistance (25%), poison (save or paralyzed for 1d4+1 rounds).

Sea Sphere (Blubble)

Hit Dice: 8
Armor Class: 7[12]
Attacks: 3 slams (1d8)
Saving Throw: 8
Special: devour riders, engulf, resist bludgeoning weapons, vulnerable to piercing weapons
Move: 0/9/18 (flying, swimming)
Alignment: Neutrality
Number Encountered: 1, 2d4
Challenge Level: 10/1400

The sea sphere (known to sailors as the "blubble") lives in a symbiotic state with other beings. The sphere's home is the ocean and it is always found near vast quantities of water. It is an odd, spheroid creature composed of a thick membrane. The center of the creature is an air-filled chamber.

The sea sphere is the color of the water where it is found, and it is luminescent in moonlight. Sea spheres see through some innate ability or undetectable magic. They communicate telepathically, and they seek out air-breathers who desire to travel underwater.

Blubbles require carbon dioxide to breathe. They can store enough of this gas inside of themselves to last for up to 72 hours. During this time, their respiratory processes use up the carbon dioxide and produce waste oxygen, which is expelled inside their inner bubbles. After 72 hours they run out of breathable gas and die within 1d4 hours. Blubbles stay alive by welcoming oxygen-breathing creatures inside their hollow core. These creatures — usually humanoids — breathe the blubble's oxygen and naturally exhale the carbon dioxide the host blubble requires.

Sea spheres can open an aperture in their shells to permit up to six creatures to enter their core. The blubble provides travel for these beings and is able to swim to great depths where the air-breathers usually couldn't venture. The blubble is not violent; however, a suffocating blubble too deep to breach the water's surface is not above forcing air-breathing creatures inside it. If too many creatures try to ride within the blubble or if they injure it (or anger it), the blubble can engulf creatures and exude acid into the inner chamber to devour the riders. Each creature within the blubble must make a saving throw or take 4d6 points of damage from the acid.

Sea Sphere (Blubble): HD 8; AC 9[10]; Atk 3 slams (1d8); Move 0 (fly 9, swim 18); Save 8; AL N; CL/XP 10/1400; Special: devour riders (save or 4d6 acid damage), engulf (save or be forced into sphere's interior, Open Doors check to escape), resist bludgeoning weapons (50%), vulnerable to piercing weapons (200%).

Storm Rider Swarm

Hit Dice: 6
Armor Class: 6[13]
Attacks: swarm (2d6)
Saving Throw: 11
Special: immune to lightning, watery glide
Move: 18 (swimming)
Alignment: Neutrality
Number Encountered: 1, 1d3+1
Challenge Level: 7/600

The fish known as a storm rider is barely two feet long, with a body wider than it is high; combined with its broad fins, this gives it an aerodynamic quality and allows it to leap into the air and glide on winds for an extended distance. The mouth of the fish is filled with many sharp triangular teeth like the blade of a saw.

Storm riders are a deep-sea fish that are relatively harmless individually, but become dangerous in great numbers.

They are most often encountered gliding in large schools in the violent winds of a stormfront, where they can descend upon a ship and ravage its riggings and crew. Ironically, storm riders are quite tasty when cooked, and they are considered a delicacy in many ports.

The storm rider swarm can leap out of the water and fly up to 60 feet each round, but it must start and end its movement in the water. If it is flying at the end of its turn, it falls, taking falling damage. If the storm rider swarm uses this trait in a strong or stronger wind, it can instead fly for up to five minutes before it must return to the water.

Storm Rider Swarm: HD 6; AC 6[13]; Atk swarm (2d6); Move 0 (swim 18); Save 11; AL N; CL/XP 7/600; Special: immune to lightning, watery glide (storm rider swarms can leap out of the water and fly up to 60ft in a round before returning to the water).

Thume

Hit Dice: 6
Armor Class: 7[12]
Attacks: stinging tendrils (2d6 + poison)
Saving Throw: 11
Special: deflect spells, detect magic, immune to poison, poison, spells, vulnerable to piercing weapons
Move: 18 (swimming)
Alignment: Neutrality
Number Encountered: 1, 1d4+1, 3d8
Challenge Level: 9/1100

A thume resembles a large jellyfish with dozens of strands dangling from the fringe of its body. The interior of its body is largely hollow, interlaced with razor-thin lines of phosphorescent energy, and many translucent organs cluster around the top and sides of its form.

The thume are an ancient race of deep-sea dwellers that evolved — or were uplifted — from large jellyfish. They bear a close resemblance to their primitive cousins but are much larger, with an obviously complex interior structure composed partly of a pastel lattice of energy.

The thume live in communities on the ocean floor, usually in well-tended sea gardens, with sculpted stone married harmoniously with carefully-placed sea flora. Thume do not sleep and have no need of houses or other conventional structures. Their "cities" are often no more complex than a large, cultivated area with hundreds of their kind dancing above it, alone or in congregations. Thume do build a few structures, however, to aid in one of their favorite pursuits — the study and use of magic. They sometimes set up forges and research facilities near thermal vents. They often recruit other undersea races, whether as hirelings or through magical compulsion, to aid in the physical process of manufacture.

Thume avoid direct combat when they can, relying on summoned or charmed minions and their arcane powers to protect them. As masters of the art of breeding, thume communities often incorporate dangerous sea life into their defenses, including giant sea anemones. This is sometimes supplemented with charmed monsters and magical traps or with their own formidable talents in the arcane arts. Thumes can cast spells as an 8th-level magic-user.

Thume: HD 6; AC 7[12]; Atk stinging tendrils (2d6 + poison); Move 0 (swim 18); Save 11; AL N; CL/XP 9/1100; Special: deflect spells (immune to 1st-level spells; +1 bonus on saves to all others), detect magic (120ft range, as spell), immune to poison, poison (1d6 damage and paralysis for 1d4 rounds, save avoids), spells (4/3/3/2), vulnerable to piercing weapons (200%).

Spells: 1st—*charm person, light, magic missile, shield*; 2nd—*darkness 15ft radius, invisibility, mirror image*; 3rd—*dispel magic, hold person, lightning bolt*; 4th—*dimension door, fear*.

TIRMANHA SWARM

Hit Dice: 6
Armor Class: 7[12]
Attacks: swarm (2d6)
Saving Throw: 11
Special: none
Move: 24 (swimming)
Alignment: Neutrality
Number Encountered: 1, 1d3+1
Challenge Level: 6/400

A tirmanha fish individually reaches 10 to 12 inches in adulthood. Its plump, jagged-edged body is a shimmering white color with deep black features on its belly and fins. The tirmanha's steep forehead, blunted face, and dominant lower jaw complement its menacing demeanor. Its mouth holds columns of razor-sharp, spoon-shaped teeth that are intended to devour wooden objects and materials but are just as hazardous to fleshy subjects.

Tirmanha are an abnormal species of piranha that have a boundless appetite for wood and hunt in swarms. The tirmanhas' prime source of food is wood, which leads them to wreak destruction upon waterbound trees, docks, and ships. Starving tirmanha swarms hunt other creatures if no wooden food source is available, though the swarm must consume twice as much flesh to get the same nourishment it would from a piece of wood.

Tirmanha Swarm: HD 6; AC 7[12]; Atk swarm (2d6); Move 24 (swim); Save 11; AL N; CL/XP 6/400; Special: none.

UNRELENTING SOJOURNER OF THE SEA

Hit Dice: 16
Armor Class: 0[19]
Attacks: 3 slams (3d6)
Saving Throw: 3
Special: +2 or better weapons to hit, healing, immune to most spells
Move: 12/9/9 (burrowing/climbing)
Alignment: Neutrality
Number Encountered: 1
Challenge Level: 20/4400

The This construct appears as a crudely rendered statue of a human, with fully-articulated joints. Though its facial features are nothing more than vague shapes with little definition, its torso is carved with an intricate pattern of runes. Along the area of its left thigh is a long, silvery abrasion, evidence of some ancient battle.

The sojourner was given its name by a maritime explorer who encountered it, fought it, and retreated with his life to tell the tale. No one knows its true name or even if it has one. It is a human-shaped machine that constantly walks the ocean floor on an unknown quest, destroying anything that attempts to sway it from its inexorable path. The sojourner is fashioned from a special, highly resilient metal of unknown origin, its power source hidden somewhere deep inside its nearly impregnable frame. It continuously and unstoppably walks the lightless ocean floor, having traversed thousands of miles since it was first spotted by adventurers years ago. So far it has proven indestructible. Its purpose remains a mystery. The symbols on its torso are as inscrutable as the sojourner itself.

During its endless trek along the sea bed, if the sojourner encounters an obstacle it cannot pass through or climb over, it walks around the obstacle's perimeter, regardless of the distance required. It descends into the deepest ocean trenches and slowly advances up the far side. If a living being attempts to impede its progress, the sojourner attacks without hesitation, though it never initiates combat until it is touched or attacked. In combat the sojourner is mindless, fearless, and unremitting.

Unrelenting Sojourner of the Sea: HD 16; AC 0[19]; Atk 3 slams (3d6); Move 12 (burrow 9, climb 9); Save 3; AL N; CL/XP 20/4400; Special: +2 or better weapons to hit, healing (acid, cold, fire, lightning damage heals equal hit points), immune to most spells.

WATER PACER

Hit Dice: 5
Armor Class: 8[11]
Attacks: bite (1d6 + poison), hook (2d4)
Saving Throw: 12
Special: poison, water walker
Move: 15/6 (swimming)
Alignment: Neutrality
Number Encountered: 1, 1d4+2, 2d8
Challenge Level: 6/400

The water pacer is a mischievous spider-like beast that glides effortlessly along the water's surface. Its

Water pacers dwell in moist dens near coastal areas and swamps but spend most their time upon the open sea.

Though their appearance is rather intimidating, hundreds of years of co-existence with native islanders has mostly removed the water pacer's aggressive behavior toward humanoids. The water pacer generally feeds on small fish and insects near the water, dipping its claws in the water and manipulating food into its mouth.

Water pacers effortlessly glide along the surface of the water. Their back three pairs of legs have a waxy, water-repelling quality that supports their full weight atop the water's surface. They propel forward with the rowing motion of their middle two pairs of legs, creating mere dimples in the water. Their back legs brace and steer the body in the desired direction.

Despite their monstrous appearance, water pacers provide faithful service as mounts to coastal, sea-fairing people. Islanders wishing to travel relatively short distances across water have long developed specialized techniques to train these creatures. Islanders sell trained water pacer mounts for twice the cost of a warhorse.

Water Pacer: HD 5; AC 8[11]; Atk bite (1d6 + poison), hook (2d4); Move 15 (swim 6); Save 12; AL N; CL/XP 6/400; Special: poison (save or 1d4 damage), water walker (can move across water like it is solid ground while carrying up to 250 pounds).

WEEDGE

Hit Dice: 4
Armor Class: 8[11]
Attacks: spear (1d6)
Saving Throw: 13
Special: amphibious, leap
Move: 12/12 (swimming) (30ft leap)
Alignment: Neutrality
Number Encountered: 1, 1d6+1, 3d6
Challenge Level: 4/120

The weedge is a froglike humanoid, quite wide in the chest but with spindly arms and legs. It is human-sized and wears a thick eel-skin belt to hold a variety of tools that it can wield in its webbed hands.

On the faraway planet of Lacosta, two races vied for control of the scant resources available. Once the kuah-lij mastered the seas with their machines and magic, the weedge were forced to fall in line. Certainly, the amphibious weedge still have havens, small enclaves that are unimportant to the kuah-lij and their ambitions. The weedge are a storied race, ranging the seas and the coastal lands alike, building cities underwater and advancing a culture of diligent and loyal people. Their wisdom and experience are unequaled on their planet but their younger rivals proved stronger and more aggressive. The kuah-lij have forced the weedge into a servile role, employing them as soldiers in the front line to repel the invaders of their mutual home. The weedge have longed served as workers in kuah-lij factories and as craftsmen and farmers in their villages. They also make up a large part of the army set to defend the kuah-lij. Their sacrifices as the front line against the invasion of their world has made the weedge a wise people accustomed to the rigors of a centuries-long war.

Before becoming servants of the kuah-lij, the weedge were artisans, scholars, and architects. After they lost to the kuah-lij, the devoted weedge refused to mourn the loss of their people's dominance and turned their passions toward bettering themselves and their equipment. They begin training at an early age, and, after reaching a certain level of expertise, they go into careers as servants and soldiers for the kuah-lij. Though trained in various weapons, they prefer the spear for its versatility underwater. The weedge serve in companies of five and fight well in concert with their teams. A group of weedge fighters that has been together for years is a formidable opponent.

Weedge: HD 4; AC 8[11]; **Atk** spear (1d6); **Move** 12 (swim 12) or leap (30ft); **Save** 13; **AL** N; **CL/XP** 4/120;
  Special: amphibious (can breathe air and water), leap (30ft leap).
  Equipment: spear.

WHALE, DEEP SINGER

Hit Dice: 18
Armor Class: 4[15]
Attacks: bite (3d10), tail (4d10)
Saving Throw: 3
Special: entrancing song, spell-like abilities, swallow whole
Move: 18 (swimming)
Alignment: Lawful
Number Encountered: 1, 1d8
Challenge Level: 21/4700

The deep singer whale looks much like a sperm whale, though it has midnight blue skin.

Only in the deepest oceans can one find the deep singers, a race of intelligent whales that sing with an entrancing harmony and that are said to be the repositories of all the sea's wisdom.

A deep singer can travel to any depth in the ocean without harm, but it breathes air, nonetheless. It is occasionally seen by sailors as it breaches the surface to replenish its air supply. Its haunting songs can be heard echoing among the waves, rising from the deeps. Its songs are of such melancholy beauty that even the most hardened sailors find tears in their eyes.

Deep singer whales are often accompanied by a retinue of dolphins and intelligent, sea-dwelling humanoids such as merfolk, who come to learn from the whales' song and bring the whale information from the world beyond. Some believe that deep singer whales are the first stage in the evolution of the celestial whales that swim in the oceans of the Outer Planes. Others believe they are avatars of those beings, come to the world to increase their knowledge and experience before returning.

Anyone within whosthe song (as the *charm person* spell)

Deep Singer Whale: HD 18; AC 4[15]; **Atk** bite (3d10), tail (4d10); **Move** 18 (swim); **Save** 3; **AL** L; **CL/XP** 21/4700;
  Special: entrancing song (120ft range, save or captivated by song as *charm person*), spell-like abilities, swallow whole (natural 20 to hit).
  Spell-like abilities: at will—*magic missile* (3d4), *protection from normal missiles*; 3/day—*phantasmal force*, *silence 15ft radius*, *sleep*; 1/day—*wizard eye*, *legend lore*.

This product contains Open Game Content, which may only be used under and in terms of the Open Game License Version 1.0a, distributed by Wizards of the Coast, Inc. Open Game Content includes all new monsters and all game mechanics (including the methods, procedures, processes and routines to the extent of such content does not embody Product Identity).

OPEN GAME LICENSE Version 1.0a

The following text is the property of Wizards of the Coast, Inc. and is Copyright 2000 Wizards of the Coast, Inc ("Wizards"). All Rights Reserved.

1. Definitions: (a)"Contributors" means the copyright and/or trademark owners who have contributed Open Game Content; (b)"Derivative Material" means copyrighted material including derivative works and translations (including into other computer languages), potation, modification, correction, addition, extension, upgrade, improvement, compilation, abridgment or other form in which an existing work may be recast, transformed or adapted; (c) "Distribute" means to reproduce, license, rent, lease, sell, broadcast, publicly display, transmit or otherwise distribute; (d)"Open Game Content" means the game mechanic and includes the methods, procedures, processes and routines to the extent such content does not embody the Product Identity and is an enhancement over the prior art and any additional content clearly identified as Open Game Content by the Contributor, and means any work covered by this License, including translations and derivative works under copyright law, but specifically excludes Product Identity. (e) "Product Identity" means product and product line names, logos and identifying marks including trade dress; artifacts; creatures characters; stories, storylines, plots, thematic elements, dialogue, incidents, language, artwork, symbols, designs, depictions, likenesses, formats, poses, concepts, themes and graphic, photographic and other visual or audio representations; names and descriptions of characters, spells, enchantments, personalities, teams, personas, likenesses and special abilities; places, locations, environments, creatures, equipment, magical or supernatural abilities or effects, logos, symbols, or graphic designs; and any other trademark or registered trademark clearly identified as Product identity by the owner of the Product Identity, and which specifically excludes the Open Game Content; (f) "Trademark" means the logos, names, mark, sign, motto, designs that are used by a Contributor to identify itself or its products or the associated products contributed to the Open Game License by the Contributor (g) "Use", "Used" or "Using" means to use, Distribute, copy, edit, format, modify, translate and otherwise create Derivative Material of Open Game Content. (h) "You" or "Your" means the licensee in terms of this agreement.

2. The License: This License applies to any Open Game Content that contains a notice indicating that the Open Game Content may only be Used under and in terms of this License. You must affix such a notice to any Open Game Content that you Use. No terms may be added to or subtracted from this License except as described by the License itself. No other terms or conditions may be applied to any Open Game Content distributed using this License.

3. Offer and Acceptance: By Using the Open Game Content You indicate Your acceptance of the terms of this License.

4. Grant and Consideration: In consideration for agreeing to use this License, the Contributors grant You a perpetual, worldwide, royalty-free, nonexclusive license with the exact terms of this License to Use, the Open Game Content.

5. Representation of Authority to Contribute: If You are contributing original material as Open Game Content, You represent that Your Contributions are Your original creation and/or You have sufficient rights to grant the rights conveyed by this License.

6. Notice of License Copyright: You must update the COPYRIGHT NOTICE portion of this License to include the exact text of the COPYRIGHT NOTICE of any Open Game Content You are copying, modifying or distributing, and You must add the title, the copyright date, and the copyright holder's name to the COPYRIGHT NOTICE of any original Open Game Content you Distribute.

7. Use of Product Identity: You agree not to Use any Product Identity, including as an indication as to compatibility, except as expressly licensed in another, independent Agreement with the owner of each element of that Product Identity. You agree not to indicate compatibility or co-adaptability with any Trademark or Registered Trademark in conjunction with a work containing Open Game Content except as expressly licensed in another, independent Agreement with the owner of such Trademark or Registered Trademark. The use of any Product Identity in Open Game Content does not constitute a challenge to the ownership of that Product Identity. The owner of any Product Identity used in Open Game Content shall retain all rights, title and interest in and to that Product Identity.

8. Identification: If you distribute Open Game Content You must clearly indicate which portions of the work that you are distributing are Open Game Content.

9. Updating the License: Wizards or its designated Agents may publish updated versions of this License. You may use any authorized version of this License to copy, modify and distribute any Open Game Content originally distributed under any version of this License.

10. Copy of this License: You MUST include a copy of this License with every copy of the Open Game Content You Distribute.

11. Use of Contributor Credits: You may not market or advertise the Open Game Content using the name of any Contributor unless You have written permission from the Contributor to do so.

12. Inability to Comply: If it is impossible for You to comply with any of the terms of this License with respect to some or all of the Open Game Content due to statute, judicial order, or governmental regulation then You may not Use any Open Game Material so affected.

13. Termination: This License will terminate automatically if You fail to comply with all terms herein and fail to cure such breach within 30 days of becoming aware of the breach. All sublicenses shall survive the termination of this License.

14. Reformation: If any provision of this License is held to be unenforceable, such provision shall be reformed only to the extent necessary to make it enforceable.

15. COPYRIGHT NOTICE

Open Game License v 1.0a Copyright 2000, Wizards of the Coast, Inc.
System Reference Document 5.0 Copyright 2016, Wizards of the Coast, Inc.; Authors Mike Mearls, Jeremy Crawford, Chris Perkins, Rodney Thompson, Peter Lee, James Wyatt, Robert J. Schwalb, Bruce R. Cordell, Chris Sims, and Steve Townshend, based on original material by E. Gary Gygax and Dave Arneson.
Swords & Wizardry Core Rules, Copyright 2008, Matthew J. Finch
Swords & Wizardry Complete Rules, Copyright 2010, Matthew J. Finch
Swords & Wizardry Monstrosities, Copyright 2013, Matthew J. Finch
The Tome of Horrors Complete, Copyright 2011, Necromancer Games, Inc., published and distributed by Frog God Games; Author Scott Green.
Tome of Horrors, Copyright 2002, Necromancer Games, Inc.
Tome of Horrors, Copyright 2005, Necromancer Games, Inc.;
Tome of Horrors© 2018, Frog God Games, LLC, Authors: Kevin Baase, Erica Balsley, John "Pexx" Barnhouse, Christopher Bishop, Casey Christofferson, Jim Collura, Andrea Costantini, Jayson 'Rocky' Gardner, Zach Glazar, Meghan Greene, Scott Greene, Lance Hawvermale, Travis Hawvermale, Ian S. Johnson, Bill Kenowner, Patrick Lawinger, Rhiannon Louve, Ian McGarty, Edwin Nagy, James Patterson, Nathan Paul, Patrick N. Pilgrim, Clark Peterson, Anthony Pryor, Greg Ragland, Robert Schwalb, G. Scott Swift, Greg A. Vaughan, and Bill Webb
Dead Man's Chest Copyright 2019 Frog God Games, LLC; Authors Lance Hawvermale, Rob Mason, Robert Hunter, Patrick Goulah, Greg Ragland, Matt McGee, Chris Bernhardt, Casey W. Christofferson, Chad Coulter, Skeeter Green, and Travis Hawvermale

www.ingramcontent.com/pod-product-compliance
Lightning Source LLC
Chambersburg PA
CBHW081329090726

47907CB00010B/2419